Bobby Truax

Denise Cassino

Long Story Short Publishing

First Printing 2022
ISBN: (Paperback)   978-0-9796080-9-4
ISBN: (eBook) 978-1-0880-3248-0
Publisher BestsellerServices.com
Printed in the United States of America

Author Disclaimer: This book is pure fiction. Any characteristics, descriptions or details such as physical properties, occupations, people or places of residence are based on the author's experiences. Any similarities to real people, living or dead, places or things are purely coincidental.

DEDICATION

This book is dedicated to my husband and partner, Lon, and my beautiful mother, Marilyn.

Acknowledgments

I want to thank all of the authors I
have worked with over the many
years for their inspiration, love,
and support.

CONTENTS

PROLOGUE

Bobby Truax felt like shit. Three days in a tent had his bad leg aching, and he was sorely in need of a shower. He'd drunk too much whiskey the first night out and still didn't feel right. He was too old for this kind of stuff but couldn't help himself. As he rounded the curve toward his gate in his rusty red pickup, the last thing he wanted to see when he stopped at the mailbox was a Sheriff's car sitting at his gate. His heart pounded and his mouth got even drier. This was it. This was the moment. He was ready.

He didn't trust cops in the best of circumstances, so he stood by the mailboxes, sorting through the pile to give himself time to clear his head and calm down. His hands weren't shaking, and luckily there was a shitload of mail there to add credence to the story he had already fabricated.

Bobby's oversized head was completely bald, but he wore a dark mustache and goatee. Beefy, deep creases ran along his thick neck and puffy eyes peered from above dark circles. A stained t-shirt, stretched tightly around his barrel chest, had pulled up slightly to expose a firm but protruding gut. He wore blue jeans and work boots, one of which had a three-inch heel and sole, and as he moved, he carried a slight limp.

He looked like a lost Vietnam Vet living a desultory life on a disability pension. His careless appearance suggested a loner going through the motions of living, drinking his nights away, watching old war movies. He was a big man, and as he stood sorting through his mail, his thick arms and broad shoulders flexed. His veteran's license plate shook as his tailpipe collided abruptly with a rut and flew off to the side of the road, leaving him unfazed. He turned down his private road with a resounding backfire and pulled up in front of his old, misshapen cattle gate and got out to unlock it. The Deputy got out, too, and introduced himself. He stood there in his dark green shirt and gray-brown pants with his patrol hat on and Bobby would have laughed if he weren't so shaken up. The guy had one of those long, skinny necks that slopes down into wedge-shaped shoulders that point downward themselves. Wiry, he had a beaky nose and looked about as authoritative as Barney Fife.

"How's it goin?"

"Fair to middlin'. What can I do for you?"

"I'm investigating a missing person. Mind if I take a few minutes of your time? He was headed this way, and I just need to ask you a few questions."

"Sure, didn't see nobody, but how can I help?"

"This might take a while. Mind if I go down to the house with you?"

This was the last thing Bobby wanted, of course, but he figured he'd covered his tracks pretty good and didn't want to arouse any further suspicion, so he said, "Sure, follow me in."

It was a decision Bobby would live to regret.

Bobby pulled slowly onto the driveway pad and the Deputy stopped a short distance back. The dogs were lying in the grass chewing enthusiastically on something, so he felt a little better about forgetting to feed them before he left a few days earlier. He watched the Deputy talking into his radio before they both got out of their vehicles and approached one another, the Deputy with his arms curved out wide, like all do, to keep from hitting all the damn paraphernalia they've got hanging on their hips as they walk. The dogs saw the cop and started to bark. That's when Bobby saw a flash of light, and he felt pretty sure the Deputy saw it, too.

The dogs were chewing on the ragged arm and hand of the revenue agent Bobby had buried three days earlier. The thumb was gone, and the index finger pointed straight up. The middle finger had been chewed down to the first knuckle and his ring finger with the glinting wedding band and pinkie were down to the second. The ring flashed gold and shiny in the light. Bobby's heart started to pound, and he froze in his tracks. Time moved like a slow pendulum, and as he looked up, the Deputy's eyes met his, and he knew he'd seen it, too. The Deputy reached for his gun and yelled, "Hold it right there!"

Bobby never hesitated a second before survival instinct took over. He spun around, ran and delivered a lunging kick to the groin that dropped the Deputy to the ground, clutching his privates and moaning out loud. The dogs converged on him and began licking his face, and he slapped at them in his agony.

BOBBY TRUAX

Robert Livingston Truax grew up in the Denver area in a small post World War II G. I. bungalow in one of the many neighborhoods that cropped up after the boys returned from the battlefield ready to marry and start families. Growing up in the fifties was the best. Kids had total freedom to play outside if they promised to be home when the streetlights came on. Most kids rarely left their block because every block was inhabited by families like Bobby's. His father was a blue-collar worker, his mother stayed at home. Few kids arrived home after school with a latchkey in their hands.

Most families gathered for dinner nightly, and the phone was not to be answered, nor were meals interrupted by a blaring television, which by then, most families had. Of course, they were small black and white console televisions around which families gathered to watch one of the shows American families grew to love. Matt Dillon dominated every scene of "Gunsmoke", "Bat Masterson" was cool as a cucumber and "Father Knows Best" always delivered a positive message.

Bobby had an older brother and a little sister, the apple of her father's eye. Bobby's mother was a sweet, wise lady who deferred to her husband's judgment on most matters, if she could stand it. Sometimes, though, she had to resist, fight back, but often that triggered a fist slam on the kitchen table, and she knew to back away.

School was only blocks away, and everyone walked or rode their bikes. It wasn't till high school when many kids rode the bus to the school a mile or so away. Walking home from school was when Bobby and his friends had the most fun. Oh, they weren't bad kids, just pranksters who pranked mostly each other, but Bobby's mother worried he'd get in trouble due to his incorrigible spirit. His kid sister, Liz, liked to tag along and as they got older, she tried to rein Bobby in a bit but to no avail. Bobby was just a wild guy, and there was no changing him. Liz finally gave in, along with the rest of the family, and just loved Bobby for who he was. Bobby and Liz were still very close, though their lives had gone in dramatically different directions. Liz had finished college, the only kid in the family to do so, and had gone on to a great career with IBM, who dominated the office machinery industry in those days.

Bobby was always a tough kid, prone to fistfights and general shenanigans, but never in serious trouble with the cops. The only really frightening experience was when he and his high school girlfriend were chased down by a cop in an unmarked car and accused of attempted murder! Apparently, the cop's son was the one in a road war with Bobby that caused the whole thing.

The father happened to see the chase and pursued both of them. When the cop's kid told him Bobby had tried to run him off the road, the cop hauled Bobby into the station. They dropped the entire case, but it left Bobby with a negative attitude toward cops. Bobby's older brother, Jim, had bailed him out and tried to explain to their father that it was all just a bad mistake. Bobby was forever grateful to Jim, who always seemed to be there when Bobby needed him most. Both boys had muscular frames like their father and worked out in the basement with weights during their teen years.

Girls always liked Bobby. He was handsome and a little on the quiet side with women. They often had to be the aggressor to get his attention. When he met Sandy, it was a little different. He was smitten at first sight. There was a quiet calm about Sandy, and she seemed to have a way of soothing Bobby when he got upset, which, as time wore on, was fairly often. It was only six months after they started dating that Bobby and Jim both got drafted.

Jim had been in community college but flunked out and the draft got him. Bobby got his notice the same month. The draft was the dreaded fear of all young men back in the sixties. If a kid wasn't in college, he was fair game and most found themselves inducted soon after graduation.

On December 1, 1969, the Selective Service System of the United States held two lotteries to determine the order in which men would be called to military service in the Vietnam war for men born in the years from 1944 to 1950. The President designed these lotteries which ran during "the draft" period—from just before World War II to 1973. Lottery numbers were assigned based upon birthdate and used during calendar year 1970 both to call for physical exams and potential induction. The Vietnam war started with "advisors" being sent to support the South Vietnamese government against the threat of communism that had been on the rise since the end of World War II.

Stalin began to conquer parts of eastern Europe, adding to the land Russia had acquired in the spoils of war. In February 1965, President Johnson began the air war, ordering sustained bombing of the North. The first ground troops entered the country to the South. A few months later, the first major national anti-war demonstration, organized by the SDS (Students for a Democratic Society), took place in Washington. By the year's end, the anti-war movement had grown to hundreds of thousands of protestors spilling into the streets of eighty cities.

From 1965 to 1970, the United States saw a deep divide in public sentiment over the war. Peace protests seemed to pop up on every campus, and activists from the civil rights movement, and other political groups joined in, inflaming the movement. The "Chicago Seven" trial electrified the country and infuriated parents and "the silent majority", who mostly supported the Washington establishment. Men were burning draft cards, and some men refused to serve, dodging the draft by escaping to Canada and other countries.

Bobby loved his country and his brother and figured if they could go in together, they'd survive. Well, it didn't turn out quite that way. They were separated. Bobby went into Special Ops, and Jim became a chopper pilot flying Medivacs out of the war zone. Both were in the thick of battle and their lives were at risk daily. Bobby made it out, but Jim's copter went down with eleven injured passengers onboard. All died.

When Bobby heard of Jim's death, something inside of him died, too. A rage began to grow in that dead place and Bobby developed an angry edge that likely kept him alive throughout his service in Vietnam. The war probably would have gone on and on—it was the longest war in which America had taken part till that time, but a Peace Moratorium on October 15, 1969, became the largest demonstration in the nation's history. Two million people marched for peace. The next month, Americans learned that U. S. troops committed atrocities in a village called Mi Lai. Finally, support for the war totally crumbled, and President Nixon felt pressure to negotiate for peace.

When Bobby returned home after his second tour of duty, it was because of a severe blast to his right leg that left it three inches shorter. America was a far different country than he'd left behind. When he shipped out, the girls were still wearing pastel skirt and sweater combos, bouffant hairdos and dark eyeliner. Guys wore their hair short and dressed in cotton shirts and creased pants.

Now, everyone was raggedy, bell bottom blue jeans had holes in the knees and hung low on the girls' hips, fringe swung from leather jackets and vests and long hair was in vogue by men and women alike. Total hatred for the war, the military and anyone who had gone over to "kill babies" was palpable.

Bobby came home without Jim, and his life was never the same. The two people who saw him through the worst of it were his sister, Liz, and his sweetheart, Sandy. His dad said little, having served for the duration of the Big War, but he saw the pain in his eyes. His mother, whose heart was surely broken, was the glue that held everyone together.

Bobby and Sandy married a year after his return. It was a small but lovely wedding. Liz was maid of honor, and Jim's absence hung in the air despite the joyous celebration. Weddings weren't quite the extravaganzas they'd once been. Many "hippies" were marrying in the forest or on the beach. Churches were taboo, and if you were cool, you did something unusual. Bobby and Sandy chose a mountain retreat with a big open meadow for the reception. Afterward, they took a small second-floor apartment of barely 500 square feet with a small kitchen, living room, bedroom, and bath. It was their first home, and they loved it.

Sandy enjoyed homemaking, but took a job at a local bank to help make ends meet while Bobby grew his construction business. It wasn't long before Bobby had three trucks, a shop and a going business that was throwing off some pretty decent cash. But he made a terrible mistake. He didn't pay his employment taxes to the Feds, and they levied his bank account and confiscated his trucks, equipment and anything else they could transport. It was a cruel blow that further jaded Bobby's attitude toward authority. Broke and defeated, they moved out of the luxury home they'd bought just after little Bobby was born and found an old mountain home they could afford near to where they married.

They were happy. At least as a happy as a man with Bobby's psyche could be. His anger emerged more often, and his hatred for the government and authority simmered at a low boil. His genuine joy came from his son. Little Bobby. He was their everything because, after a difficult birth, Sandy was unable to have any more children. Little Bobby adored his dad and traipsed alongside him as they walked through the hills and forests. Bobby had spent months in physical therapy to reach a point where his leg injury was a nuisance at times, but little more than that. Most people didn't even notice with the built-up sole on his one shoe that evened out his stance.

JOHN TREMONT

John Tremont had just survived the hellish experience of a divorce, the inevitable result of a marriage that never should have happened, but after Vietnam, seemed like the right thing to do. He'd dated Marlene in high school for two years before he shipped out, and she was good enough to write to him the whole time he served "in-country." That alone deserved some consideration, since letters were about the only thing that kept most of the guys going—letters from home and especially from a woman. He read and re-read those letters until they fell apart in his hands, and in the course of it, she became a fantasy, a dream woman whom he loved deeply—a woman he could fight and die for. After he came home to post-Vietnam America with the anti-war movement in full stride, it seemed she was the only person who cared or understood.

He may not have survived the days of being called a "baby-killer" without her at his side. Some things people said and did pierced his soul, but they survived the baby-killer era. A year later, they got married in a big, full-blown church wedding. They produced a couple of great kids together, but sadly, after the initial interest wore off and the sex slowed down, they realized they didn't have a thing in common. They were more of an irritation to one another than anything.

Oh, they stuck it out for twenty-four long painful years, fussing and fighting and gnashing their teeth, growing further apart by the day. Why they stayed together, neither will ever know, but most likely it was for the kids. They were both extremely proud of their kids, grown-ups now, but once they left, and they only had one another across the room, things got really grim. They tortured each other for a few more years until neither could take it any longer. Then they set about studiously inflicting some last punishment during the divorce. In the end, they split the equity in the house, divvied up the worn-out furniture and gratefully went their separate ways.

Now, John was fixing to move into the mountains to get as far away from her as he could and to heal his wounds in private. Like a lot of other Colorado folks, he always wanted to live in the mountains, but with the way life is anymore, it's just about impossible with kids. They're involved in so damn many outside activities, a fellow spends half his life delivering a mini-van filled with noisy kids to or from lessons of every kind—piano, dance, equestrian, tennis, soccer and team sports like soccer, little league and basketball. They spend the other half sitting on hard benches, cheering optimistically as his six-year-old barely avoids a death by trampling during a soccer match.

Sometimes you have to wonder how today's kids will turn out. Their parents seem to have gotten by nicely hanging around the backyard torching ants with a magnifying glass or playing pickup softball on a vacant lot in the neighborhood. Even when they played Little League, they rode their bikes to the games, and if their folks came, that was great, but it didn't matter. Now, most parents even attend practice. But who's to criticize other people's activities? Many people like John spend half their time lying on a scruffy sofa watching sports or sitcoms on television. John spent the rest of his time rebuilding an old backwoods cabin that was likely to kill him if I didn't go broke first, but that he somehow thought would be a fun project.

Anyway, the day John first saw Bobby Truax, he had driven the dirt roads around Long Bow and seen the For Sale sign. Being a curious bastard, when he saw this property that lay somewhere beyond a gate offering nothing but wide-open spaces for as far as the eye could see, he got a hold of the lady realtor who listed the property and asked to have a look at it. He parked near the mailboxes and saw Bobby come through, driving into that open space. Then the realtor showed up.

When she pulled up in a Mercedes SUV sporting all the bells and whistles and climbed out wearing a thousand dollars' worth of clothes on her back, John had to rethink his life choices. Is the market that good? She wore a leather suit with matching boots and bag, enough jewelry to bond out Charles Manson and her walk made you wonder if she'd been in the saddle all night. Oh, she seemed nice enough and was good to look at, and so he followed her right on down the road to the old place.

Fool that he was, he bought it on sight. It sat on the southern edge of Long Bow, came with forty acres and an old ranch house, and had a real good asking price - the kind of prices before they blew sky high when they widened Highway 285. He had to admit, Charlene, the realtor, moved around the mountain pretty well for the way she was decked out. She scrambled her way into the stand-up crawl space, mixing right in with the spider webs and the wide assortment of materials probably gathered by a family of pack rats, one of which he later met face-to-face in the dark of night. All in an effort to help him check out the underpinnings and so-called systems. Those "systems" consisted solely of an old hot water heater, which, incidentally, blew a month after he moved in.

Then, they climbed the hill and looked at the roof. The place had been a seldom-used summer cabin, complete with a shower stall lined with asphalt roofing, the entrance to which sat side by side with the toilet leaving about nine inches of clearance. The shower was kiddy-corner from the sink, and they were all in 18-inch proximity. It's the only place he'd ever seen where you could sit on the john, wash your feet in the shower and brush your teeth in the sink all at the same time. The kitchen, which had always been an unfamiliar room to John, was spartan, but adequate. Four small upper cabinets - two metal, two wooden - graced the wall above the tiny 1935 Westinghouse electric range. Next to that sat a heavy piece of plywood covered with oilcloth, which provided the base for an old, oversized sink. Many people used to have that kind of sink - about three feet across with a wide sink on one side and a built-in drain board on the other. The faucet sat high above it all. He liked it. A five-foot tall Coldspot refrigerator, the kind where a couple of inches of ice would build up in the tiny freezer, completed the ensemble of antique appliances. An old, blue enamel kitchen cook stove, turquoise actually, sat diffidently in the corner, having retired from its once important duties.

The place looked pretty quaint and old-fashioned, and it had that smell of a musty cabin that conjures images of yesteryear. It just seemed to grab John right by his ready ass. But the best part, as though the previous list was a positive one, was the utter isolation of the place. You couldn't see another house in any direction - just Pike's Peak softly shrouded in a stole of pale clouds with surrounding peaks ranging in colors of deep purple to pale lavender stretching miles into the distance. Guess he got caught up in the magic and overlooked the negatives—like the wind blowing through the exterior walls and the abundance of holes in the roof. For a fifty-year old guy, he could be pretty dumb sometimes.

Of course, John was not alone. Every guy that ever went camping Rockies in thinks the mountain life is for him. Many newcomers, especially Californians, talk their wives and families into moving up without a clue of how hard mountain living really is, what with the firewood, cold winters, short summers and all. And the dirt—no one tells you about the dirt, but outside of the front doors is mostly dirt that gets tracked in with every trip, along with chips of bark from the loads of firewood that must be hauled in each day for heat.

The old hardwood floors in John's place had seen better days, and he knew he'd probably have to refinish them at some point, but right now, with the other work to do, he also knew it would be foolish to start there. He was pretty sure he'd live out his life in the old place, but lots of families only last a couple of years. By then, the wife is so fed up with the hardships, she divorces the old man and splits with the kids. It's not a life for everybody. Too bad so many people have to learn that the hard way. The result is that there's a pretty big turnover, so those folks who stick it out become well known, if only by sight and local lore. That was the case with Bobby Truax, until, of course, he finally became a real folk legend.

Face to Face

J ohn got to know Bobby because he had to pass
through his gate to get to his place - that and their
both being Vietnam Vets, which he mentioned as an
icebreaker when he actually spoke to him.

John had a theory about Vietnam Vets. Many people
think the war destroyed those men or at least changed
them into the walking dead or made them into deadbeats
of some kind. He disagreed. He thought the way they
went in is the way they came out: good or bad, crazy or
sane. Vietnam just exacerbated their condition. Oh, no
doubt it was a grueling, terrifying, dehumanizing
experience—war always is. Fact is, John saw a lot of
action over there, but when he got out, he put it behind
him as best he could and moved on.

That's not to say he hadn't had an occasional nightmare
or that it hadn't entered his thoughts every day of his
life since, but it hadn't ruined his life. He didn't have
flashbacks or any of the other devastating side effects
that some guys have, and it hadn't made him hate the
government or the folks who run it.

Too many guys constantly relive the war and can't find
another thing in life that's quite as stimulating. John had
to admit, it was definitely the experience of a lifetime, but

there's more to life than an adrenalin high punctuated by sheer terror followed by boredom. When he got back, he found his cheap thrills in more conventional ways like water skiing and snow skiing and such. He moved on like most of the Vets did. Some guys, like Bobby, carried the detritus of war along with them for life, like empty cans dragging noisily behind the cars with "Just Married" scrawled on the rear windows. The war affected John deeply, but he just didn't make Vietnam into his sacred shrine - it was what it was.

When he prepared to close on his place and move in, of course, he had to arrange for gate keys, and for that, he had to make Bobby's acquaintance. He left a note on his gate, telling him he had bought the old place and hoped to be a good neighbor. John asked if they could get together to exchange keys and general information. He called back pretty quick.

"John Tremont? Bobby Truax."

"Yeah, Mr. Truax, glad you called me back so fast. I've bought the old Brown Place. Wanted to make your acquaintance and work out a way to get a gate key."

"No shit! You bought that place! You're one brave son of a bitch! Goddamn! It'll be nice to have a neighbor, though. When you moving in?"

"Well, I close on the twenty-third and should move in by the first."

"You and your family?"

"No, just me. I'm divorced and my kids are grown."

"Yeah, okay."

They talked a minute or two, and John asked him if he'd been in Nam. He said yes and Bobby's voice perked up right away. Then he invited John on up for a get together the next day.

John got off work and drove the fifteen miles up from Denver and stopped at the gate where they met and Bobby waved him in through the battered old Cyclone gate. He followed him down to his place, which sat in the middle of a beautiful meadow. He said the original owners had cleared the land and harvested the logs for building the place back in the forties.

Apparently, the Corps of Engineers had built it through some kind of connection the original owner had. It looked solid, from what John could tell. Fall had left his enormous yard area with heavily overgrown buffalo grass, browned and standing two feet high.

Dry leaves littered the area and weeds proliferated amongst a variety of dead wildflowers, poking their tattered heads out here and there. Now, bear in mind, most mountain folks don't have a real yard with grass like city folks.

Nevertheless, this appeared to have been a well-groomed place at one time, with stone walls, terraced hills and rock-bordered garden plots, none of which were still maintained. I found out later that he bought the place from an old couple who'd kept it up with flower and vegetable gardens and trimmed grounds and such, but when John saw it, it grew wild, kind of like Bobby himself.

Bobby met John with a broad smile before he even got to the door.

"Bobby Truax," he said, holding out his hand to shake.

"John Tremont."

They shook hands, and John noticed the size of his hand - like shaking hands with a bear. A couple of mutts of questionable and indiscernible breeds had barked ferociously when John first approached until he calmed them down with a little dog talk. Now, they were lying about diffidently, chewing intently on the sawn-off leg of what appeared to be a freshly killed elk judging by the dark brown fur and hooves. Elk season didn't start for another month, so John wondered if he'd poached it.

The remnants of trash and empty cat food cans lay strewn amongst the weeds and a big dog food bag had blown up against the hillside and left to fade in the sun. He stepped over the sundry pots and pans scattered about the yard, which held water and a variety of dog foods including spaghetti and something unidentifiable, which he chose to ignore.

"Nice place you've got here," John said generously.

"Yeah." He gazed out over the area. "I don't do much with the yard, but, hey, it's the mountains anyway. Who needs grass, know what I mean?" He laughed and stroked his beard.

"Come on in. It ain't much, but it's home." He chuckled.

"Thanks."

They walked up the stone steps to the small, enclosed porch where a shiny black cat sat on a carpeted, homemade perch, licking its paw and paying no mind whatsoever. Bobby rubbed its head, and it rubbed back, purring loudly.

"Good kitty, good little kitty, aww, you're so good." Bobby seemed genuinely attached to those animals.

A lot of junk lay in piles inside the little porch - bags of pet food, shoes and boots and some boxes and old, rusty, odd tools. When John got inside, he saw painted shelves containing antique coffee and tobacco cans and an old oil lamp. Couldn't feature Bobby as much of a collector, so John assumed they must have come with the place.

The house appeared to have changed very little over a twenty or thirty-year period judging by the outdated furnishings and shag rugs. The walls wore mahogany paneling, and heavy, flowered drapes covered the windows. In his good-sized kitchen, John could see he'd done the dishes by hand. Most folks in the mountains don't have dishwashers, and John didn't expect Bobby would require that luxury.

An endless bottles of vitamins lined his shelves, which surprised John. He wouldn't have taken Bobby for a health nut of any kind, especially given the bags of potato chips and sweet rolls on his countertops. The rest of the place he kept neat and organized, which seemed out of character given the condition of the grounds.

Oh, he had a lot of stuff around, but he had stacked it in neat piles around the rooms. He had some military and gun owner magazines, and John spotted some survival manuals. One side of the hearth had a stack of newspapers about a foot deep and the mantle still sported last year's Christmas cards in prominent display.

It was obvious that Bobby didn't need to be on the cutting edge with his décor. He had a thoroughly lived-in household with an outdated but unique character. Little did John know how intimately he would become acquainted with the old place."

"Have a seat." He nodded toward a table in front of his massive fireplace, which had a toasty blaze that warmed the room nicely. He opened the refrigerator and popped the tops on two cans of Coors regular, offering one to John. Ice cold, it felt good bubbling down their throats.

Then Bobby banged a quart bottle of Jack Daniels down between them and grabbed a couple of shot glasses. He looked them over pretty good and wiped them out with a dishtowel. He poured two shots and slid one toward John. "To Nam," he said. They both tossed it back with a grimace.

Bobby wiped his mouth with the back of his hand, snorted and sat down across from John. He dug in his pocket and pulled out a bag of pot, thick and green. He plopped it on the table like an announcement. Didn't bother John. He was used to that shit. He looked up as though to get a nod, and John gave him one.

"Don't indulge myself anymore," John said. "Not since Nam, but don't mind if you do."

He rolled a joint, talking idly as he grabbed a magazine, laying it out on the table. He reached into the bag and pulled out a nice fat bud, which he crumbled with his fingers onto the cover. Using the thin cardboard edge of the Zig-Zags, he scooped up the pot and let it pour back onto the tilted magazine. The seeds rolled to the bottom leaving the sticks and stems in the middle. He picked them out and spread out the rest breaking up the big clumps.

Using one rolling paper and shaping it with both hands, he sprinkled the cleaned pot into the paper, poking it around with his huge forefinger to distribute it evenly. Then, he licked the glued edge and quickly rolled it up and sealed it, twisting both ends a bit. He held it by one end, stuck it in his mouth and pulled it back out through his pursed lips to seal it a little more.

Then he leaned back in the chair and relaxed while he lit the joint, holding the flame there until the twisted end burned away, puffing until the weed caught fire. Feeling good, he dragged deeply, holding the smoke in.

"Sure, you don't want a hit?" he asked in a raspy voice, blowing out a plume of acrid smoke.

"No thanks, man. They do mandatory drug testing at work."

"Oh yeah? Where do you work?"

"I'm in quality control out at Lockheed Martin. I work on the Atlas Project."

"No shit? That must be a pretty cool job. You work on those rockets?"

"Yeah, the ones used to launch satellites—you know, like weather satellites, cell phones, government stuff, too."

He nodded and took a long drag and tapped the joint on the edge of a little tin ashtray, losing the ash. Then he looked at the tip and took another hit. I figured it must be a way of life for Bobby.

As he smoked, he sat back and looked John straight in the eye, telling him about the history of his place and how an old doctor had built it back in the forties. He seemed to think the doctors and nurses used it as party spot back then. To hear him tell it, those nurses gathered often for what sounded like hot sex parties, and I thought it might be just hearsay—you know, local lore.

"Yeah, you got your hands full fixin' that place up, I'll say that."

"No doubt," John said. "It needs a lot of work, but I figure I'll tackle the toughest first and work my way down. It needs insulation badly."

"Insulation? It needs everything, Bro," Bobby said, laughing, and John started to wonder if he'd bitten off a tad too much. He had to admit to worrying a little. A little? Well, maybe a lot. He hadn't slept much the night he signed the contract, thinking about the potential nightmares he faced. He tried to assuage his concerns by remembering that he could be starting with a patch of dirt rather than the shell of a cool, old mountain lodge.

"It's been sittin' mostly unused for years. The old guy's kids used to come up once in a while, but nobody's much cared about that old place since I've been around these parts. Couldn't ever figure out why. We kids always loved it. We used to break into it once in a while when we were younger, before we moved up here. Our grandparents lived not too far from here, so we poked around most of the old places as kids."

"So, you kind of grew up here?"

His eyes narrowed like he needed to think about it a little to recollect or maybe he was just getting stoned. He flicked the lighter on and off four or five times before he spoke.

"Oh, my grandparents lived up here when I was a kid. Used to spend summers at their place, but I've been living in the hills since '75 in one place or another. I had a place up Sunrise Trail, the old Frederick's place—lost that in foreclosure in '78, though, thanks to the fucking IRS. Anyway, I don't know, I guess I always wanted to live up here. Just something about the solitude and, of course, the views. I don't have much of a view from here, though. Your place has got the best of that."

John thought about the dark pine-covered mountains lying south of his place and the view of Pike's Peak. It made him feel a little better. He took a swig of his beer and stared into the fire for a few minutes. As he waited for Bobby to continue, he looked around and noticed one picture on his mantle. In it, a small boy sat in Bobby's lap. He looked like a regular guy in the photo. No beard then, still had hair, though it was thinning. He waited silently, since it seemed like he had more on his mind, and John had plenty of time to listen, kind of interested, in fact.

"I made the mistake of bringing my wife and son up here. Like a fool, I bought the first place I saw on sight, the one at the top of the road with the view of the Divide. You know the one I mean?"

John said he didn't, but began to wonder if he'd been the same kind of fool.

"It's just a little place, not much, way at the end of the road, but the views are incredible, man. That's where I saw my first UFO, in fact."

His eyes narrowed at the recollection, and he took another hit. John had to believe he embellished a bit, but he wasn't about to call his bluff, so he took the bait.

"Your first? You've seen more than one?"

"Seen a bunch," he said, nodding sagely. "Just keep your eyes open up here on moonless nights. You'll see them—be surprised at what's out there. Lot a folks think they're just seein' shooting stars or satellites, but they're wrong. They're amongst us." His voice wavered, and he leered at me.

John nodded, wondering if he had gone a little bit whacky, but gave him the benefit of the doubt.

"So, after you got foreclosed, then what?"

"Well, I wouldn't have stayed. You know, the wife wasn't too happy, at first. I think she got to like it more after a while, but I was kind of a dumb shit, the way I uprooted her and the kid. I mean, we had a hell of a nice joint down in suburbia. I know she liked living down there. But I fell in love with the place, so I just went home one day and told her to start packing." He shrugged and took a swig of his beer. "I fucked up." His already bloodshot eyes narrowed, but John thought he saw them get a little teary, too. Funny, a guy like that—you'd think he had a heart of stone, but deep down, he's a marshmallow.

"Didn't go over too good, huh?"

"Nah, but Sandy handled it better than most women would. See, I knew her throughout high school, so I don't think I surprised her much with anything I did. I think I was kind of both her father and her husband. Her old man was a total dickhead. He left the family when she turned fifteen, but made sure he beat her and molested her for a few years before he left. Goddamn miracle she came out as good as she did. So, I suppose I looked pretty tame and safe." He tilted his head quickly to one side. "I think I took good care of her."

"You still friends?"

"Oh, yeah. We're actually seeing each other again, and we talk every few days or so. Lot a bad shit went down, and that's what ended it. I think she still loves me, and I still love her, you know." John nodded.

Bobby picked the roach out of the ashtray with two fingers and fired it up for a few more tokes before he got up and opened a couple more beers. The light had grown dim, and he turned on the fluorescent light in the kitchen, flipping on the TV without the sound for the light, John figured. Clearly, ambience was not his forte. He sat back down and leaned into his chair, and John got the feeling he was just getting started.

"Sandy is a good woman, really." John looked at him and waited. Finally, he asked, "How so?"

"Well, we met in high school, went steady, all the typical bullshit. I remember she always wore my class ring wrapped in some kind of fuzzy yarn that matched whatever color she wore that day.

"Neither of us did much in school. Hell, I barely graduated, but she always got decent grades, though she never joined no clubs or nothing that I can remember. Seems like she spent all her time with me."

John took a sip of his beer and nodded again. He'd known lots of girls like Sandy. Their entire life wrapped up in their boyfriends and later, their husbands. Sometimes it works, and sometimes it doesn't. They either go a little nuts around age thirty and need to "find themselves" or they end up married for life. Just depends on the people.

There's a theory called The Half-Full Cup. It goes like this: if a person is a whole complete person, fully developed and mature, his cup is full and overflowing. He has extra to give to a spouse, kids, family and friends. But if he is not a whole person, still "finding" himself, his cup is only half full, and he spends his life trying to fill it, always taking, having no extra to give. They are what we call nowadays, "Me" people. Me, me, me is all they can think about because the cup is only half-full. You rarely find a full cup person involved with a half-full cup person. It's too draining, taxing. It takes too much out of a person to always give and never get. But two half-full or two full cups and can get along great. They understand one another. The half-fulls end up doing all of that crazy stuff like walking the hot coals or attending EST meetings or spending years of their lives and thousands of dollars in therapy. So, that leads back to Sandy and women like her.

Turns out, she must have had Bobby high up on a pedestal like a God or something. So, she hung around, biding her time, while he enlisted in the Marines and went off to Vietnam for two tours of duty.

"You re-upped?" John asked shaking his head and smiling knowingly.

Bobby grinned almost shyly and rubbed his shiny head.

"Shit, man, you know how it is when you're that age - just couldn't get enough." His voice rose a bit in pitch.

"Finally, I became a so-called casualty of war and spent four and a half fucking months in a VA hospital with my leg in the air and a bunch of other fucked up dudes laying next to me moaning for hours on end. They had all kinds of tubes and shit, bedpans and colostomy bags. One guy lost both arms and a leg. That was the worst part of that fucking war. That's when I got this limp."

He lifted his leg, and I saw the three-inch heel and sole of his boot. "But you know what? I might have stayed longer if that hadn't happened. Lost three inches of bone." He nodded solemnly and patted his thigh.

"Whew, that must of have been a bitch," John said, and meant it. He'd seen too many good men with devastating injuries and screwed up for life. Sorriest thing you'd ever see. He shook his head in sympathy..

It turns out, Bobby had been a volunteer combat engineer in Vietnam – a Tunnel Rat.

"They took me and my squadron by helicopter into enemy territory. I used to ask myself what the hell I was doing there whenever I got in a tough spot. I'd look all around me and see death lurking right over my shoulder, leering at me, and I'd shudder. But not too long, and I couldn't wait to get back out there - go back for another dose – you know, get some more of that old magic elixir - that adrenalin rush, huh?" He peered at John from under raised eyebrows as he took a sip of his beer.

Oh yeah, thought John. I knew the adrenalin rush alright – he had to admit the rush was so powerful, it felt like fire shooting out your fingertips. That seemed to be the case with many of the guys over there. Living on the adrenalin rush, waiting for the next fire fight. Some of them got to the point where they thought they were invincible and did a lot crazy shit, just pushing the envelope, defying the odds. Some of them made it, some didn't. Everyone saw a lot of dead GI's and even more dead Gooks.

"Me and my team were moving into an area where the NVA had an endless maze of underground tunnels - the things ran for miles. Our mission was to find all the entrances, get the intelligence, plug 'em up and blow 'em - suffocate those bastards. I had located some entrances when a sniper in the trees opened fire and blew my thigh in half." He patted his leg.

His team managed to get him to a clearing to where they could Medivac him out, saving his life. The shot had severed his femoral artery.

"Man," John shook his head. "Not many guys live through that - once the femoral artery is hit."

"No shit. I lost about half my blood, but somehow I got lucky. Lucky. Yeah – just another lucky break." He shook his head with half a smile. "I'd say I've had quite a few of those so-called lucky breaks."

"Once they put my leg back together, it ended up shorter than the other. They gave me this built up sole, and shit - it works pretty good."

"Still have pain?"

"Oh, just once in a while if I get real tired, it'll pain me some. This usually takes care of it." He lifted another shot of Jack and grinned, tossing it back. "Don't like to take those painkillers or pills everyday. Liquor and pot – my drugs of choice. Bad thing is, I still dream about the medivacs – whup, whup, whup. I wake up with that sound of the copter blades in my head. Whup, whup, whup." He tipped his head and raised the empty glass in salute.

John had started to like this guy for some strange reason. A unique character, and yet so much like a lot of guys he had known forever. So, he kept going on and on about his life story. John had the feeling he didn't get out much anymore.

"My little brother died over there. Shot down his Huey. Couldn't find enough of him to send home. All we got were his dog tags and a box of his stuff."

He lowered his eyes as he spoke. John winced. Bobby stood up and pulled a dog tag off a nail he had in the wall and tossed it at him. It said "James Thurber Truax."

"Wow, James Thurber Truax," I said admiringly. "A literary buff in there somewhere. "

John turned it over in his fingers and so many memories, both good and bad, flooded back. He shook his head and handed it back to him. "Bummer, man. Lot a good guys died over there."

Bobby nodded gravely. They both drifted back for a moment to those days in the bush when guys only had each other. Lying in the dark, under that black, starlit sky, wondering about home, wondering if our women were waiting for us or getting it on with some other guy. Lots of the guys had babies, some they never saw. Those memories live forever with those who were there, half-buried somewhere deep in the darkest places of the soul, emerging daily when little things like a walk in the woods or the sound of a gunshot or a pair of dog tags brought it all back in an instant rush. Overall, it seemed Bobby sorely missed the war, though he felt betrayed by the government for putting us there in the first place if they didn't want to win it outright.

"Too Goddamn bad LBJ didn't do it right. Or maybe that asshole McNamara. Anyway, seems we were doomed from the start and didn't even know it," Bobby lamented.

"Yeah, I know what you mean. Remember when we heard those broadcasts with Hanoi Jane? Those pictures of her on that anti-aircraft gun? Shit, the stuff I've learned about how she and all those protestors extended the war, giving those assholes hope that we would pull out. Makes me sick. I'm still getting over the way we were treated when we got back. I remember I was on the plane coming home – still in uniform. I sat next to a woman and her kid. She told the stewardess she wanted to move to different seats because she didn't want her kid exposed to a baby killer. Man, that ripped my guts out." How many times had he told that sorry story?

John shook his head and remembered back, back to that sinking feeling in his gut, that anger that surged when someone saw him in uniform or heard he'd fought in Nam. Bobby had lived through it all, too, but it seemed liked he'd suffered more or at least didn't put it behind him as well.

Then, he got onto the government and what bad guys and liars they all are. How there's a big conspiracy out there to bamboozle the American people, keep us in the dark.

Everything from Ruby Ridge to Waco pissed him off, and John could relate to some of it himself.

"Much as I don't like his method, I do understand Timothy McVeigh's madness. He just took out the wrong people. He should have hit those folks in Washington. Just too bad he killed the kids, that's all. But I have to agree that somebody has to stop the boys in Washington – I say boys because the way I see it, most of those broads back there have a hard on, too, and besides I don't go in for all that women's lib bullshit anyway. Power crazy, that's what they all are. They don't give a shit about the folks out here in flyover country. McVeigh was just trying to make a point that they work for us, not the other way around – our rights are being constantly eroded." He wouldn't live to see the incredible erosion of American rights that would follow in subsequent decades.

"Yeah," I agreed, "but even that paled in comparison to the 911. I'll be glad when this election is over - so much dirty pool. These guys are ruthless. Do they ever think about the common man?"

"Well, I don't even vote anymore – pure bullshit!" He dug the roach out of the ashtray and held it between his ragged fingernails, tilting his head to one side as he tried to light it. The flame danced dangerously close to his nose, but he finally got it to light, took a short hit, and slumped back in his chair with relief while a thin cloud of pungent smoke encircled his head. "Reminds me of the time I talked my mom into taking a hit, way back when. She was pretty funny. We were sitting in our family room when I pulled out a joint. I took a hit, gave my brother a hit, and he passed it to Mom. She looked at the roach and said, "Put that dirty thing out and light another one.""

"Your mom still alive?"

"Nah, both Mom and Dad died years ago."

"Mine, too. I miss them."

Bobby nodded and gazed out the window.

John had to agree with him to the extent that he also believed those Washington folks had lost touch with the ordinary American. What to do about it? That's another thing altogether. That's when he told me about all his trouble with the IRS.

"I had a construction company for awhile – I was doing real good, too. I had about nine, ten employees, a few trucks and a shop. When I got behind on my payroll taxes, they started hounding me day and night. I tried to work something out with them, but those folks are real serious about payroll taxes. Next thing I knew, they emptied my bank account just before they pulled up outside my shop and padlocked everything. Then, they drove my trucks away! They left me with nothing, except the bill for the difference I owed them in taxes. I pretty much gave up after that. What's the point, you know? They're still after me for what I owe, but I just ignore those fuckers. Let 'em come and get me.

"Worked a few odd jobs after that, but by then, Sandy and Bobby were gone, and I didn't really give a shit. Applied for disability with the VA and haven't filed taxes since."

John wondered what happened to his kid, but he figured he would get around to that eventually without his asking. So, he just nodded politely, trying to commiserate as best he could, given that he didn't completely agree or disagree, though he could understand his attitude. Then he started in again, this time about the aliens and UFO's.

"I'm not shitting you, man. I see them all the time in the skies above the hills - big, bright lights, just hovering up there. They get pretty close at times. Some nights I climb up on the roof and just lay up there waiting - got to do it on the darkest of nights, you know. If you get a big 80,000-candle power lamp and a laser light and shit, you can definitely call them in close. I figure it's just a matter of time. That's where I'm coming from – I'd like to go off with them. You know they've got civilization on other planets. It's just pure logic, man! Probably wouldn't have to put up with so much bullshit up there neither. Think they've got an IRS?" He laughed a little bitterly and hefted another shot.

He went on to say our government is really missing the boat on new technology, life-changing type of stuff he believed, by not communicating and engaging the extraterrestrials. It really pissed him off that the government had lied to us about their existence at all, and he was trying to do something about it.

"I found a group that's trying to change all that – to force them to disclose what they know. They've been lying too long - ever since Roswell, man! They've still got those bodies in the warehouse somewhere but won't admit it. Hell, there's so much evidence of ET's that it's unbelievable, but they keep it all hidden from us peons. They think it'll scare us, we won't be able to take the shock. It's pure bullshit." He stroked his beard and mustache.

His eyes were seriously bloodshot by now, and his eyelids were heavy, but he still didn't slur his words. He was a regular human dynamo.

"Why can't they just admit it? We know there are plenty of documented sightings; they just won't let folks talk about it. They're sworn to secrecy. Jesus Christ – this is America! What happened to freedom of speech? Freedom of information? So, we're all sending emails and writing protests all over the world to our leaders and others. We want 'full disclosure' – nothing less."

Seemed he had a real fixation on the subject.

John drank his beer and gave his thank you and stepped over the dogs on his way out, but he knew he had a friend and, be that as it may, he knew he could count on him in a pinch.

Hanging with Bobby

W hen John moved into his place, he faced the hard fact that he had taken on a whole lot bigger project than he had ever intended or originally thought. The place needed serious help. He just about went broke trying to get it insulated in time for that first winter and still liked to freeze to death. Every night for a month, he lay on his back on top of some rented scaffolding, trying to get the ceiling insulated.

One morning in January that year, he woke up and the temperature had dropped to twenty below and going lower. It finally bottomed out at 28 below. Frost had formed in the corners of the kitchen, and grown to an inch thick, like in the old freezers before they were self-defrosting. John set to stuffing every crevice and crack with insulation, but the wind still whistled through in icy drafts. It took him that whole winter to tighten the place up with a truckload of insulation, sheets of Visqueen and barrels of caulk.

That same week he'd gotten an invite to go down to Denver for a party on Saturday, but by mid-afternoon the weather turned nasty. A blizzard raged by five that evening and the temperature still lurked way below zero.

John thought better of heading down the mountain, even though his vehicle could handle it just fine.

Fact is, he had no desire to get caught in the skating rink that develops in Turkey Creek Canyon at night during a nasty blizzard. Cars are spinning and careening into each other and running off the road into ditches. They end up stranded sideways on the center line and begging for a tow. It's hard to say no and before you know it, you're in it with them. No way. No thanks.

So, he stayed in, built a big fire in his living room fireplace, a pretty efficiently designed massive rock structure, considering its age or maybe even because of its age. He sat up close to the fire munching a bowl of popcorn and drinking a rum and coke when he heard a funny sound—a kind of hissing. He shook it off as another weird, old-house sound and kept on watching the tube. Little while later he got up to take a pee and the fool bathroom stood an inch deep in water. The shower pipe had burst from the cold. He got the main valve shut off and mopped the place up.

Next morning, he had to cut out the split pipe and sweat a new section in its place, something that became a struggle, especially in the numbing cold. At that moment, he gave serious consideration to a remodel of the bathroom. Another thirty-minute job. He chuckled. It was an old joke—every time you think something's going to be quick and easy, just a thirty-minute job, apply the formula—multiply by ten. In this case, he knew untold nightmares lay in store for him, hidden behind those old walls – what walls there were, but hell, those days he didn't have much else to do in his spare time. At least not yet.

Between the house and work, a job that had escalated into more than he had in mind when he'd signed on at Lockheed Martin - he was suddenly running a department and working lots of overtime -- it was at least a month or two before he ran into Bobby again. He dropped in one day when he was changing the oil on his

Ford pickup and his buddy, Tim, stood around with his thumbs in his back pockets.

John got the feeling a pretty good time usually unfolded around Bobby no matter what was going on. So, the beer started flowing, and they got to talking about marriage and other bad shit. This guy intrigued him. One thing led to another, and they started telling him about Bobby and Sandy's wedding. It turns out, Bobby and Sandy got married up nearby in the hills.

"I'm not much into religion, myself," Bobby said rolling out from under the truck. "Hand me the 9/16ths wrench, Tim."

Tim put his cigarette in his lips and dug in Bobby's toolbox with both hands.

Funny, a lot of guys who survived the hell of Vietnam went the other way and became born-again Christians, but not Bobby.

"So, when Sandy and I decided to do the deed, I just couldn't get next to a church wedding." His muffled voice came from under the car.

Tim laughed a little and his pale blond hair shook like corn silk.

"They got the idea to have the wedding at a friend's place in the hills, not too far from here. We were all for it. I mean, shit, people flew in from all parts, and Bobby and Sandy put on a hell of a mountain bash."

John could tell this was one of Tim's finest memories, and he'd told this story many times before.

"Just one of those awesome summer days – not a cloud in the sky. You know, the perfect Colorado bluebird sky?" he asked.

John nodded. He was talking about a cloudless, deep, blue sky from morning till night that takes your breath away. It is one of the most amazing things about living in Colorado. The aspen leaves shimmer and quake in the breeze and the fresh mountain fragrance intoxicates.

He learned somewhere along the line that the reason aspens "quake" is the way their stems attach to the branch. Most leaves attach in a vertical parallel way and aspens attach in a kind of horizontal, perpendicular fashion, which makes them twist and turn differently as they blow.

"They got married in a backyard area a lot like this." He swung a hand toward the yard and looked out at the ravages of Bobby's yard as though seeing it through fresh eyes.

"Well, maybe a little better than this, huh, Bobby?"

He laughed hard and then coughed, pounding his chest before taking a medicinal drag of his smoke.

"Had a regular ceremony, lot of chairs set up and a flower arch and all. Then, after all the formal stuff, cake cutting and the like, everyone partied in this big-ass meadow nearby. They had kegs of beer and cases of champagne, and we partied all day and night. Bobby was in the bucks back then. Ain't that right, Bobby – "Workin' for the man every night and day!'" he sang out, laughing and tapping Bobby, who had rolled out from under the car, on the leg with the toe of his boot.

"Remember that band?" Bobby asked, using a dirty rag to wipe grease off his hands, finger by finger. He clearly enjoyed this.

"Yeah, what was their name again?"

"Summit, they were called Summit. I still have the posters we stenciled their names on so they could find the place."

They'd found a little known but talented band who agreed to come up the mountain and play their tunes, powered by a noisy generator which they hid in the aspen grove that their even louder music managed to drown out.

"I'm telling you, they could play everything from Billy Joel to Jimi Hendrix. That meadow rocked hard all day long. You know, they even played for a couple of hours longer than we hired them for, but I gave them a big old tip. Sandy about killed me, but it was worth it. They were really good. As I remember, they left for a European tour the next day. Everybody danced in the field and Sandy, still in her white dress, put on her black flip flops and pinned up the brim of her hat, and had a good old mountain time."

They fed the guests on barbeque, beer and champagne, and after dark, they built a big bonfire and the revelers gathered around and sang songs while everybody indulged and imbibed till the wee hours.

"You should have seen Sandy. There she lay, passed out next to the fire in her wedding dress wearing someone's old jacket, and Bobby, superhero that he is, picked her up and carried her to the car. Shit, she still remembers it as the best day of her life, doesn't she Bobby?"

Bobby just blinked and looked sadly resigned. It was clear he missed her, and I hoped they could work it out.

He took Sandy straight home afterward since they had already moved in together, but I guess more than a few people camped out or just landed face down in the field, and they said the party went on for a day or two more, at least until the kegs were empty.

"Folks raved about it for years - saying it was the best wedding they'd ever been to and all that kind of shit." His eyes rose upward at the memory as he nodded and took one last drag off the butt of his cigarette before he tossed it to the concrete floor and crushed it with his boot.

John got the feeling those were the best days of their lives, and nothing ever really came close again. It had been a steady decline ever since, and it seemed Bobby just got more aggravated by the day.

CHRISTMAS

C hristmas came and went, though John didn't have so much as a wreath on the door. Oh, his kids found time to come up one afternoon before Christmas, and they exchanged gifts which, when it came down to it, amounted to them giving him a couple of things he had little use for, and him giving them money. Dana arrived first. She walked in with her mouth wide open and stared around the living room in apparent disbelief.

"Daddy! You live here? I can't believe it. You don't even have walls." She gazed in amazement at his R-19 wallpaper. Her cheeks were rosy with cold, and she wore her long, dark hair tucked inside her winter coat. She looked a lot like her mother, only prettier. His heart always fluttered when he saw her, his baby. She dropped her packages on the old sofa and spun around as she unwrapped her wool scarf from her neck and pulled her gloves off one finger at a time, stuffing them in her coat pockets.

"How are you going to finish it?" She looked at her father as if he had gone insane, with a touch of sadness in her eyes. "I've got a plan, Sweet Pea. Takes time though, and energy, and your old man doesn't have much of either anymore. "She turned and walked toward him, arms extended. She gave him a warm hug and a kiss on the cheek.

"I'm sorry, Dad. I see the potential. I do love this enormous fireplace," she said, running a hand across the ragged rocks. "And the loft. Is that where you sleep?" She looked up at the edge of the loft where he had stacked books and such.

John nodded and started to answer when the usual boisterous arrival of David interrupted them.

"HO HO, Merry Christmas, you two." He came through the door grinning, carrying a shopping bag from Foley's. A sure sign of new shirts.

"Merry Christmas, David!" Dana headed toward the door and shared a warm hug with her lanky older brother. "Dad and I were just talking about his new home." David set down his packages and brushed his hands through his blond hair, which looked freshly trimmed.

"Dad, this is so awesome," David said, holding his arms out. "It's the dream mountain cabin. I'd give my left nut for something like this. Too cool." Dana rolled her eyes and smiled.

"Thanks, Dave. I figured you would approve." They shook hands and man–hugged. John showed them around the place. By the end of the tour, they both had a greater appreciation for what the old man faced.

"The view is outstanding, Daddy! I see how you fell in love with it. I just hope you don't kill yourself fixing it up."

"You and me both, Dana, you and me both."

John had chilled a bottle of champagne, which he made a big deal of popping, which they sipped while opening gifts. True to form, David had gotten him two new golf shirts and Dana had found a splendid book of photographs by Fielder showing awesome shots comparing Colorado scenery a hundred years ago and now - a beautiful book. He knew it took some thought.

He stood and tossed the crumpled wrapping paper into the fireplace and said, "Okay, let's head out. I'm taking you to lunch at an authentic saloon."

They piled in David's new Explorer and turned down Elk River Road, which winds through an ever-narrowing canyon populated on either side with rustic cabins, many 75 years old or more. Cabins of the kind you imagine in the Adirondacks. Tucked into the woods along the river with little bridges built for access and front porches adorned with wicker, now covered over for winter.

As they approached a sharp curve near the end of the winding river road, a funky old joint appeared. The place looked just like an old western saloon, front porch and rail for tying up a horse and a long, shiny bar inside. A sign across the front read "The Bucksnort Saloon." They fashioned the barstools from logs standing upright, smoothed and sanded on top to fit one's behind, with a shortened branch left down low for a foothold. A wood stove sat in the middle of the small dining area and threw off a good bit of heat. Burgers and burritos were the standard fare, so they ordered, and all had a margarita.

"Daddy," Dana started, licking the salt from the rim of her huge frosty Margarita glass, "do you ever miss Mom and the old days?"

"Sure, Sweetie," he partly lied. He actually did miss the family part of it, "but things just changed between me and your Mama. We're all better off this way. No point in living in misery." She nodded sadly and then tried to prop me up with a smile.

"You do seem pretty happy, Daddy." He squeezed her hand and smiled.

"That's because I've got you two." David lifted his glass in a toast and said, "Amen. Merry Christmas, you guys." They clinked their glasses together and finished up. John paid and David insisted on getting the tip. They all piled back in the car, riding silently, lost in thought. At home, John kissed them goodbye, thanking them profusely. "Merry Christmas," they all yelled as they drove away.

They had to hurry on to other commitments, like all young people, and after that, it seemed like any other day. John made himself a plate of spaghetti with Prego sauce for Christmas dinner, watched "Miracle on 34th Street", and crawled into bed early. He couldn't complain. The kids had turned out well and had both taken up residence in Denver. David owned a townhome and struggled toward his master's degree in computer science. Dana lived with her boyfriend of two years in a little house in a south suburb. She had a decent job in a law firm, and her dad expected she might marry the guy eventually, though he didn't know if he thought that good or bad. He hadn't spent enough time with him to get a handle on him, and at that point, he felt too tired to make much effort. One thing he'd learned is that time has a way of working most things out.

As for Bobby, they waved on those occasions when they passed on the road.

Fire Away!

A round the beginning of June, John drove in and Bobby spotted him, waving him onto his property. When he pulled into the property, Bobby came out of the back door with two cold bottles of beer, one of which he handed to John. Bobby knew how to keep his visitors around for a while. He wore a holster with a pistol and said, "Watch this." He turned and fired at a can on the fence and blew it ten feet in the air.

John smiled his admiration. "Nice shooting, mind if I give it a try?" Bobby grinned like he hoped he'd ask. John set his beer on a flat spot on the ground and took the gun. He aimed at the next can in a long row of them and hit it dead-on center. Bobby looked at him and nodded his own approval. They stood there and shot off the box of ammo he had outside, each shooting a full clip at a time.

"Let me show you something," Bobby said and headed toward the house, indicating John should follow. That's when he opened the safe where he kept all the guns. He had a fucking arsenal in there, and some of it illegal. John knew he had earned his trust when he showed him that stuff because God knows, he could have gotten into some serious trouble with the automatic weapons he had hidden away. He pulled out the AK-47 and the H&K

models 12 and 20. He handed John two loaded banana clips for each one. They went out in the back and Bobby rummaged around in the garage and brought out a big, black trash bag filled with empty cans, beer mostly.

"I usually take my trash into town and pitch it in somebody's dumpster, but haven't gotten around to it yet," he said as he lined up fifteen cans along the fence. They fired those rifles for an hour, and it was easy to see that Bobby loved every minute. He kept loading and reloading. He breathed deeply like he couldn't get enough of the gunpowder. I love the smell of napalm in the morning.

Turned out, Bobby had more than his share of trouble over guns, and even the death of his son hadn't ended the fascination. Trespassers were one of his problems and, in truth, everybody in the mountains had some kind of trouble with them. It seems Bobby's property was laid out in such a way as to encourage an inordinate amount of unwanted hikers. His property spanned a couple hundreds acres and right down the middle, there lay a nice, wide creek bed that ran the length and worked its way down to a small waterfall, Since water was scarce, it gave rise to a whole host of uninvited visitors hiking their way along the path for long sojourns. Well, Bobby didn't take too well to that since he lived up there to avoid other folks as much as anything.

"So, I took to shooting this shotgun into the sky to warn them off. It worked pretty well, and most folks just split once they knew they were trespassing. The trouble is, they just don't get why we won't open up our property for everyone, thinking we have so much that we should just share. Goddamn socialists! What they forget is they bring their friends, then their friends bring more friends. Pretty soon we got strangers wandering all over the place and back here, we need a little security. I mean, a fellow could die back here, and no one would know it for days. Remember the Clutter family? Crying shame. Anyway, we try to keep them all out. So, one day I picked on the wrong people. Couple of broads."

"Little while later, two Deputy Sheriffs in black SWAT gear with Kevlar vests and the whole bit showed up, banging on the door, calling out, 'Sheriff's Department, come on out' like I'd just murdered the President or something. They were pressing their noses against my old metal screen and peering in, demanding I answer their questions."

Bobby said he stood in the half-open door and explained the situation as calmly as he could given they were sweating and panting from the long hike in and mad as hell to boot, shouting their questions in his face.

"We have a report of someone here shooting at hikers. Do you know anything about that?"

He admitted to firing into the air and explained his dilemma and the frequency of the trespassing events.

"Have you reported the trespassing to the Sheriff's Department?" the blond, cocky deputy asked with a snarl.

"No sir, I haven't. My experience has been that by the time the authorities arrive, the culprits are long gone. I'm not trying to hurt anybody, I just warn them off the property the best way I know how."

Well, they read him his rights.

"Are you arresting me?" he asked. They said not yet, but he'd be hearing from the District Attorney.

Then they asked about his gun.

"Where is the gun?"

Bobby motioned over his shoulder, and they pushed past him and located the gun lying in its sheath on the back of the couch.

"We'll have to confiscate this weapon. Where were you shooting it?"

Bobby pointed toward the hill above the garage. They both turned and scrambled toward the hill like they were going after a serial killer. They returned carrying three spent shotgun shells and took those into evidence, too.

It seemed like the cops didn't have enough real crimes to keep them busy. It reminded him a little of that song, "Alice's Restaurant."

Months passed and Bobby heard nothing. He was beginning to hope it would all fade away. Finally, he got a summons to appear. It turned out they were seriously after him, and the broads got two other neighbors to join in the complaint. Bobby didn't stand a chance. Had to hire a lawyer, went through a three-day trial with maps and all kinds of exhibits and witnesses and a twelve-man jury ended up hearing the case. They said afterward that though they sympathized with him; they had no choice but to convict.

"That's the way the law works. Ain't no justice involved," Bobby said with a shrug.

The conviction required that he do a bunch of community service—sixty hours. That proved no small feat since Bobby really never wanted any part of community, but he got it done just the same, working for the forestry service part time for a couple of months. After that and the big fine they hit him with, not to mention about six grand in attorney's fees, he spent a couple of years on probation. He had to lay low and behave himself for a while. Bobby didn't like cops much in the first place, but this incident had intensified his feelings into a deep hatred for law enforcement of any kind.

"Fuckin' cops, man, always in your face. Petty shit, too. Never seem to be there when something serious goes down. Just for that kind of shit." His blue eyes flashed in anger.

Bobby ran his hand over his bald head as he talked. He might have gotten a pass on the whole deal, but he had a record of minor scrapes and trouble and a reputation for having a short fuse – road rage and such. He never passed up a chance to get in some kind of altercation, verbal or otherwise. It took little either—a tailgater too close or a guy cutting in front of him with short notice.

He usually won in those situations because of the way he acted. He'd go nuts yelling and cussing and calling them faggots and such until he had them pretty freaked out. He believed it best if people thought him to be just a little bit crazy, and consequently, they usually backed off. It must have given him a sense of power that he otherwise lacked.

The day Bobby showed John his weapons, he walked him into the den, which lay just off the living room. The old house had been built on grade, and he had cut a hole in the wood floor and dug himself a floor safe. It was about 4⅟ x 6⅟, and the hardwood flooring acted as a lid, which he raised by a handle recessed flush into the wood. He had lined it with a metal box he'd welded and hinged with another lid that had a padlock on it. He sunk it into the ground, and when he lowered the wooden lid and pulled an area rug over it, you couldn't tell it was there. The vast array of weapons was all perfectly maintained and encased in sheaths. He had hundreds of rounds of ammo with a gas mask and bulletproof vest in there, too. John had to laugh and said, "Bobby, you expecting World War III or what?"

"Hey man, you never know what to expect. I like to be prepared for anything. I've even got a year's supply of canned goods and dry food stashed away, too, just in case. You won't laugh when you have to move in with me to survive. You'll have to bring your own beer, though," he chuckled. "I have a generator, too."

Well, each to his own, John figured. It didn't make any difference if he built himself a moat, so long as he had a bridge when he needed it. John had never had that kind of paranoia, but judging by Bobby's reading material, he could see he was heavy into the siege mentality.

A Little Partyin'

Then on a Friday evening during one of those late March spells when it seems like winter is ending early and the temperatures gets up around seventy degrees, John was on the couch watching the hockey game when the phone rang. Bobby had invited his ex-wife and a buddy and his wife over to a barbeque the next day and wondered if John wanted to come up. He said the temperature might reach seventy-five degrees. John had plans to stain his deck the next day, but accepted the invite, glad for the company. He didn't go out much. Oh, once in a while he'd hit the bars with guys from work to watch a launch or something, but his social life left much to be desired by most people's standards.

It surprised him when Bobby called. He didn't seem to socialize much either, but once in a while he got a wild hare and did what he called "a little partyin." Everyone knew it turned out to be a good time and proved to be as much of a party as John had been to in the recent past.

After staining his deck that morning, he showered, pulled on clean jeans and a polo shirt and headed up the road toward Bobby's, arriving about three o'clock. Two other vehicles sat in the driveway - a red F-250 with a dent in the tailgate and a Toyota sedan. John had walked up from his place carrying a twelve pack, which he hoped somebody could keep cold. He'd asked Bobby earlier if he could bring anything and, although he said no, John brought a bottle of wine along, too, just in case.

He tapped on the door, which barely closed because of a broken spring or something. He heard him yell, "Come on in!"

John walked into the kitchen and saw Bobby leaning against the cabinets with a long-neck Bud in his hand. He offered his exotic, gang-style handshake, complete with high-fives, fist bumps and shoulder slaps, kind of a rite of passage, he learned once he became an accepted member of his inner circle. John looked around and found himself among what he figured for some of Bobby's old high school friends.

"John, meet my wife, Sandy." He hugged her to him. "Ex-wife," Sandy added. "Nice to meet you."

John nodded, "Nice to meet you, too, Sandy." Bobby was right. Sandy was a looker with long blonde hair and a still-nice figure. They shook hands.

"This is Chuck and Nicky."

Chuck stood to shake hands. Nicky averted her eyes and greeted him. John wondered how they ended up together. A tiny thing with long, black hair, she had a white streak in front. He stood about 5⁄8⁄ and was almost as wide - not so much fat as barrel-chested. He had thick, bushy blond hair that stood out in a wide halo around his head. They both wore jeans and flannel shirts.

Sandy dressed more city girl, designer jeans and a fancy top.

"Hey, man. Bobby tells me you're the dude who bought the old Jerome place, huh? Yeah, we used to party hearty down there. Remember breaking into that place, Bobby?" Chuck grinned, lifted a mostly full bottle of Gilbey's vodka to his lips, and drank liberally, wiping his lips with the back of his hand.

"Yeah, remember those chicks we brought up that time. Ooo-weee, they liked the dick, didn't they?"

Bobby laughed, and John flashed uncomfortably on the stained mattresses he'd found upstairs when he moved in.

Nicky pursed her lips and sucked on her beer bottle.

"Yeah, we had some parties there, man." Chuck offered Bobby the vodka, and he drank, too. Seemed Bud Light was Nicky's drink of choice.

"Hey, Sandy, let me put this beer somewhere cold." John handed her the twelve pack, and she shoved around the ice in the cooler to make room for the bottles. They all walked outside, and Chuck started playing tug o' war with the dogs.

He figured out pretty quick Chuck kept Nicky off limits. She was likely of the same ilk as so many women. Groomed to stick around the house and take care of their men - guys so tough, but so insecure. He learned that night that Sandy had hung in with him pretty good, even though that first year in the mountains was a real tough one.

"It was pretty bad. I tried hard to make the best of it, but the old place he bought was just plain Spartan, even worse than yours John, if that's possible," Sandy said.

Chuck turned to me. "The main floor wasn't bad – had a bath, bedroom, kitchen and what folks nowadays like to call a great room, except it wasn't all that great." He elbowed Bobby.

"Oh yeah, it had the cathedral ceiling and all and a view of the Continental Divide that would blow your mind - the sole reason Bobby bought it in the first place. But face it, the kid had to climb down a ladder into the unheated lower level. Shit, the cold forced Little Bobby to use a sleeping bag just to survive – even in summer! Bobby thought that worked just fine, but it seemed like Sandy grew more negative by the day." Sandy shrugged and shook her head.

Chuck had a long mustache than hung over his top lip, and he had that habit of pressing the whiskers down with his forefinger to nibble the ends of his whiskers. He looked at Bobby for affirmation.

"It wasn't that bad," Bobby said, shrugging and tossing the ball for one of the dogs.

"Yeah, well, not until the first time it snowed twelve inches," Sandy said, grinning.

"Sandy's Taurus just wouldn't make the hill. So, there she was climbing uphill for about a half mile in a snowstorm dragging little Bobby and carrying groceries and all. I mean, who wouldn't be pissed? In the dark yet! Bobby finally broke down and got her a decent mountain vehicle and hell, by then, most women would've been long gone. But not Sandy, she put up with it for quite a while longer."

"Yeah, too long!" Sandy said

Sandy might have put up with the mountain, but John got the feeling she was one of those chicks who got married too young and only figured out later that she might have missed out on some living. By then, little Bobby had started grade school, and she was bored to death. Chuck said she begged Bobby to let her go to work, to do something. Finally, Bobby broke down and Sandy got a job at the Eagle's Talon Grill and Saloon. She wasn't trained for anything else.

"You know the place, John, just up the road a couple of miles on the south side?" Chuck asked, pointing with his thumb.

"Must we tell this story again?" Sandy groaned.

"Yeah, I know it," John said. It had a reputation as a rowdy country bar and the local hang-out of bikers and rednecks looking for a good time. It surprised him that Bobby let her work there at all.

"She only worked three nights a week, and I think she made some decent tips. "Course that meant Bobby had to stay home and take care of the kid. One Friday night, little Bobby slept over at a friend's house, and after a few shots of whiskey, Bobby here got a bug up his ass and meandered on up to the Eagle's Talon and took a seat at the bar."

"Yeah, but he didn't tell me he was there," Sandy said.

Bobby walked up as we were talking, taking a long toke on a reefer. He handed it to Chuck who grinned at Bobby and said, "Telling him how you helped Sandy quit her job at the Talon." Now Chuck laughed hard, and Bobby got a little red in the face but laughed, too.

"Now, I've got to tell you," he said, looking at me, "Sandy was a looker back then—not bad now. But then, she was built like a brick shithouse and had a face to match. No offense, Bobby. "

True, her long blonde hair, blue eyes and high cheekbones were still beautiful.

"Bobby found a spot at the bar and just watched."

Bobby handed Chuck the reefer, and he took a long hit and held it out to me. I held up my hand to decline.

"Bobby, grab me another beer out of the cooler, will you and give this reefer to Nicky?" Bobby walked out toward where Nicky tended the grill. Sandy had provided the rest of the fixins.

When he returned, Chuck grabbed the long-neck Coors, twisted off the cap and drank deeply before he continued. I don't know how they kept going with all the drugs and liquor, but somehow it served as high-octane fuel for them.

"Sandy moved from table to table laughing and tossing her hair like a schoolgirl," Bobby said.

"I did not!"

Tim added, "He got all agitated watching, but sat still, drinking shots. Finally, when the guy at the table near the fireplace grabbed her ass, Bobby lost it. I guess he leaped across the bar room and kicked this dude off his chair with his bad foot!"

"The good old days," Sandy said wryly.

Now Chuck started laughing really hard, slapping his knee, and John couldn't help but laugh, too.

"To hear tell, he bloodied the guy's face and strangled him. He was pounding his head on the floor when the crowd pulled him off and helped the other guy to his feet. That's when Bobby grabbed Sandy by the hair and shoved her out the door and threw her down in the parking lot." He sucked his beer.

"What'd you say, again, Sandy? I love this!" he said, looking at me for agreement, face alight with pleasure.

Sandy screamed, "I said, Bobby, what the fuck are you doing? This is my job, you asshole!"

"And Bobby says – now, this is great - 'It ain't no more, you bitch, now get in the car before I kick your ass!'

"And that proved the end of our marriage and my waitressing career!"

We all laughed, even Sandy, and Bobby poured shots around. He cast a quick glance at Sandy who winked at him. I hoped that was good sign for their relationship.

Just then, Nicky said the ribs were done and dinner was ready, so we all sat down at the old picnic table to eat. Sandy had thrown a sheet over it for a tablecloth for which they felt deeply grateful, having seen the dogs languishing on top of it on more than one occasion. Nicky had cooked up a batch of sumptuous, barbequed ribs dripping in a succulent sauce. Chuck sucked his fingers and managed to get quite a bit of food in his mustache and streaks of sauce on his face, and Nicky kept looking at him, wiping her cheek and brushing her upper lip to let him know. John asked for a corkscrew from Bobby, which took him about five minutes to locate, and poured everybody a couple of inches of wine in the jelly-jar glasses Bobby provided.

"Real tasty, Nicky," John said. "You, too, Sandy. Thanks."

"Thanks, the ribs are from Tony's Meats in Arvada – they're always amazing."

"What's your secret, Nicky?"

"I simmer them in water and vinegar for two hours."

"Well, it's the most tender and tasty I've had," John said, meaning it.

She bowed her head toward her plate, long hair hanging down like protective sheets on either side of her face. They jawed for a while and all had seconds, sucking the tender meat off the bones. The sweet corn was the frozen sort, but not bad at all, and she'd made a great salad. When we finished eating, John offered to help Sandy and Nicky carry the stuff into the kitchen while Bobby and Chuck went into the garage to throw some darts.

"Great ribs, Nicky," John said, stacking two plates and shoving the empty wine bottle under one arm. He grabbed the breadbasket with the other. "You and Sandy really put on a spread."

"Thanks, I miss the mountain barbeques, but you don't have to help. We're used to doing the dishes by ourselves," Sandy said.

"No, you go relax. You dragged all that food up here."

"Yeah, we'll clean up – that's fair," said Nicky.

"Okay, thanks so much!" She flipped the dishtowel to John and went out to the garage with Bobby.

Nicky washed and John dried and pretty soon she got to talking about Sandy and Bobby, and that's when he learned that the real end of Bobby and Sandy's marriage came soon after the bar episode. Supposedly, "it" happened when Bobby and Little Bobby were out in the garage together one day.

"I don't know exactly what happened. I guess nobody does but Bobby. From what Sandy said, they were out there cleaning the guns one night." She nodded toward the garage. "She hated that Bobby always had the guns around the boy, but Bobby was real proud that his son knew about guns and for being a real man, though he was only a little kid - just ten at the time."

John nodded solemnly as he dried a plate and slid it into the cupboard.

"Little Bobby was such a sweet kid, too."

She shook her head, and he saw the look in her eyes as she thought back. She stood still, gazing off into a place he couldn't go as she pulled idly at the neck of her shirt.

"Broke my heart when I heard. I guess Bobby handed Little Bobby his 9mm Glock and said, 'Load it and shoot it at the bullseye." Bobby had a wall in the garage that he built so it'd take the bullets without ricochet."

John looked out the kitchen window toward the garage. He could hear them laughing through the open window while Sandy picked up around the yard and gathered the remaining items. The sun had slipped over the mountain and an amber glow bathed the woods. Then, he looked back at Nicky, and had a sick feeling that he knew what was coming.

"Little Bobby took the gun and the clip, loaded it, and flipped off the safety. They say he had his hand on the trigger when he started to drop the gun 'cause of its weight and little Bobby wasn't a very big kid anyway, and somehow it flipped around. He tried to grab it and shot himself in the chest. He died before Bobby could get to him. Sandy said she found them later, big Bobby laying next to the boy, holding him tight against him, kissing his hair and crying. She moved out a week after the funeral. That was the saddest funeral I've ever attended. Everybody cried through the whole service and Bobby didn't leave the graveside for hours."

John shook his head sadly and noticed a tear roll down Nicky's cheek, which she wiped away with the damp dishtowel.

"I think Bobby died a little bit that day, too, and never did get over the pain and the guilt. Ever since then he's been kind of a hermit up here. He just pushed the rest of the world out. And by then, a lot of the old crowd had moved into the city and Bobby lived mostly alone up here on the mountain. Chuck and I moved up a few years later. I guess we're probably his best friends now."

"Was there an investigation of any kind?" he asked, thinking about all the crap they put people through nowadays when there's a gun accident.

"Yeah, but the police cleared him. Called it an accident and no charges were ever brought. I think Sandy still loved Bobby when she left, and I think she still does now, but she just couldn't take anymore. I hope they can work it out and get back together, but that's a lot of stuff to get over."

Just then Sandy entered the kitchen to say goodbye. John felt really bad and had to swallow hard. We did the usual "so nice to meet yous", and He watched out the window as Bobby met her at her car. The talked for a few minutes till suddenly, he put his arms around her, and they kissed with an extended hug. Bobby watched wistfully as she pulled away and, at that moment, John had an idea of what made Bobby so angry and rebellious. Life had served him a shit sandwich.

No Mas

O ne day John ran into Bobby at the post office.
    "Hey, John, what's happening. Haven't seen you around."

John thought Bobby looked more tired than usual, but it was just a passing observation, and he thought no more about it.

Over time, John had gotten to know Bobby and some of his friends. They regaled him with a story about a closed-circuit fight at the DU arena. It was the famous "No Mas" fight. Popular and handsome Sugar Ray Leonard was a superstar, and Roberto Duran was a complete badass. A lot of folks thought they were two of the best boxers of all-time. They'd fought three times that decade. Their second fight, known as the "No Más" fight, went on to become one of the most infamous bouts in the history of boxing. It was a great fight, and the crowd was going nuts when, in round seven, Leonard taunted Duran. Leonard's most memorable punch came late in the round. Winding up his right hand, as if to throw a bolo punch, Leonard snapped out a left jab and caught Duran flush in the face. In the closing seconds of the eighth round, Duran turned his back to Leonard and quit, saying to the referee, "No Mas." Well, the fight ended there, but the night was still young.

The crowd was pissed and felt gypped and everybody in the arena was a little agitated over it. Feeling cheated and unfulfilled since the fight had been such a bust, they all drove over to the College Inn for some brews and male bonding. Tensions were high and testosterone flowed freely along with plenty of whiskey and beer. They wandered back toward the game tables, and Bobby laid his quarter on the foosball table, indicating he would play the winner. He waited around and drank his beer, but when that game ended, the loser just kept on playing.

Bobby interrupted, "Hey, what are the table rules here?"

The guy said, "There ain't no table rules, asshole."

So, Bobby reached across the table and grabbed the guy by the throat and squeezed hard.

"I'm not an asshole," he snarled into his face, spit flying. Bobby's veins were bulging in his forehead before he dropped the guy and walked away.

That was another one of those incidents that led to Bobby being a legend in his own time. Guys talked about it for years with deep admiration.

Moving on Up

Tom Wafer had already collected more this month than the others in the department and more than he had ever done before. He was due for a grade promotion, which would put another fifty bucks a week in his pocket. He'd gotten the hang of this job and collecting taxes came more easily. He felt powerful for the first time. People respected the IRS. In fact, most people downright feared the IRS. It gave him a muscle to flex that he otherwise did not have, and he relished it.

Tom's small stature was no longer an issue like it was in high school, where he competed with the jocks and their little snippy cheerleader girlfriends. The big shots' mocking laughter tortured him throughout school, but not anymore. Back then, they all thought it great fun to bump into him, knocking his books to the floor or tripping him in the cafeteria so he would drop his lunch tray of food. Then they'd all hoot and holler and clap as he scraped his lunch off the floor with the help of a few sympathetic girls. He suffered through the humiliation, resorting to activities like running for minor offices, joining debate club and working in the ticket booth for games. When he graduated, he discovered that college was much better. He'd attended a big school - Colorado

State University - and lost himself in the crowds. The dorm housed other guys just like him, and he felt like he had found a home. No, he wasn't popular, as popular goes, but he'd carved his own niche, made a few good buddies and even gotten himself a great girlfriend.

He and Carolyn both lived in the same dorm, and he'd first seen her in the cafeteria where they both worked in food service. They worked dinner together, and he had not paid her much mind until she pulled off her serving cap at the end of their shift and her red hair tumbled down her back in blazing waves and ringlets. When she turned around, he smiled, and her freckled face lit up.

"Whew, glad that's over. I'm starving. Have you eaten?" he asked.

"Not yet, you?"

"No, let's grab a tray."

They sat at an empty table. He watched her pale, delicate hands as she ate. You couldn't call her outright pretty, but he found her quiet femininity appealing. Her golden lashes brushed her cheeks and green eyes blazed in outrage as he related the horror stories of high school. They began meeting for most meals, and he learned that she, too, was a junior still living in the dorm as an RA, resident assistant, which meant keeping order on the floor and getting a free room without a roommate in return. She'd grown up in southwest Denver and had attended his sister school – Lincoln. He'd gone to Kennedy. As the baby boomer's kids grew up, Lincoln had grown so large it split in the 1960s and from it grew two rival schools. Carolyn had graduated in the top ten percent of her class while Tom had only made the top fifteen in a class of 800, but it good enough to get him into college. The rest was up to him.

Grades were important to both of them, and they had started meeting at the library to study three nights a week. Things just took off from there. He took her home for Thanksgiving, and his mother fell in love with her. That's when Tom realized he loved her, too. She treated his mother so sweetly, helping with the cooking, the dishes, sitting at the kitchen table with her chatting about mostly unimportant things, but she seemed so willing to go out of her way to be kind.

Tom's father had died of lung cancer three years earlier and that left just Tom and his mother. He felt a certain responsibility to take care of his mom and Carolyn understood that completely. In fact, Carolyn insisted they go home every couple of weekends to help and check on his mom and make sure her own family was doing okay. Carolyn had two younger sisters whose flaming red hair matched hers, and she protected them like a little mother hen. Her parents had married late in life and were quite a bit older than most of the other kids' parents. They were already nearing retirement. Her father spent his life as a supervisor in a furniture plant and had a tough, wiry build. Her mother had worked in the post office for 23 years, which would give them good health care and nice retirement benefits when the time came.

Carolyn felt especially close with her dad whose red hair matched that of his daughters. He was a quiet man of few words, but when he spoke, his words meant something. Carolyn took his advice to heart when he said, "Marry an educated man, and you'll be comfortable all your life." Neither of her parents had a formal education, but were both avid readers, and she admired their erudite intelligence and wisdom. She so wanted to make them proud and fulfill their dreams for her, even though her dad was gone.

Tom had always been studious, finding comfort in the books with which he surrounded himself, dreaming of far-off places and adventure. In his mind, he was able to reach the heights and be the man he'd never really be in real life – a Walter Mitty of sorts.

Somehow, Carolyn's growing love for him made him feel stronger and more important than ever before in his life. Tom was a virgin when he met Carolyn and was proud to discover she was, too. Their tentative explorations of one another had grown bolder and more passionate, but Tom respected her and did not want to push her into anything. One night, Tom sat across from her in the library studying his accounting and felt her stockinged foot slide up his pants leg. He gulped and looked at her through hooded eyes. She grinned slyly and her green eyes sparkled under pale gold eyelashes as she pretended to stare at her book. He looked back down. She did it again. He could feel himself getting hard. He looked up again and she winked, her beautiful white teeth shone in a full smile.

"Let's go," she whispered.

Tom did not need to be asked twice. They stuffed the books into their book bags and hoisted them onto their shoulders. The beautiful spring night was redolent with the heady fragrance of new mown grass and freshly budding lilacs wafting through the night air. As they walked down the library steps, Carolyn took his hand. He squeezed, and she squeezed back. As they walked across campus, his slipped his arm around her shoulders and pulled her close. His heart beat a little faster than usual. As they approached the dorm, she said innocently, "Want to come up?"

Until the late 60s, dorms were segregated men from women. It was strictly taboo to sneak a lover into the dorm. So the boys resorted to "panty raids." They had little or no curfew, but the girls had to be in the dorm by 10pm. So, heady with spring fever, the boys would get a rowdy gang together outside the girls' dorms shouting "Panties, panties!" The girls would respond by tossing undies out the window. My how times have changed.

Carolyn unlocked the door, and they entered her darkened room. Dropping their book bags, they came together in a clinch and found one another's mouths, twisting and turning their faces, lavishing kisses, breath coming hard.

She pulled him toward her bed and stripped off her sweater. Her blouse followed. Tom had kicked off his shoes and began dropping his pants when he stopped.

"Are you. . . are you. . . ."

Carolyn reached in her bedside drawer and pulled out a small foil package.

"I was a Girl Scout. I'm prepared," she said, grinning coyly.

Tom pulled off his shirt, and she dropped her slacks to the floor, stepping out of her shoes and socks. They stood there looking at one another – she in her plain, white cotton bra and high waist panties, him in his tightie-whities. Carolyn reached for him and pulled him down on the bed on top of her.

"Am I too heavy?"

"Not at all." She slid her hand down the front of his shorts and felt his throbbing shaft. He trembled at her touch.

Getting the condom on proved to be the toughest part, and they both shivered at its cold wetness. She went rigid as he tried to enter, and he stopped.

"Am I hurting you?"

"It hurts a little, but don't stop."

"Are you sure this is what you want?"

She nodded and kissed him. He pushed forward, and she went rigid again, clenching her teeth at the pain, but urged him on and rode it out. Afterward, they lay spent, and he asked, "Was it okay?"

"It was beautiful."

"You're beautiful," he sighed, snuggling close.

Tom gave her an engagement ring at Christmas of their senior year, slipping it on her finger during the enchantment of midnight mass. They were married the following June in a joyous ceremony held in her family's church. The reception was a catered affair in her parents' backyard complete with a makeshift dance floor and Chinese lanterns.

The bride and groom chose the George Strait song, "I Cross My Heart" for their wedding dance, and they held each other close, gazing into loving eyes. Many who attended the wedding said they'd never seen a couple more in love. They found a small apartment in Lakewood and soon were happily ensconced in marriage. By September of that year, they were settled, and Carolyn took a job teaching first grade while Tom reluctantly went to work at H&R Block as a tax preparer. It seemed a little unrewarding after the pain of earning his degree in accounting, but he hadn't taken his CPA certification yet and had to settle for what he could get. The pay was marginal, but it gave him some good experience. Two years later, Tom became a CPA, studying long nights to make sure he would pass the test first time around. Carolyn had been so sweet, bringing him tea and handling the household chores so he could study. She usually had homework herself, so they spent their evenings quietly together.

Finally, Tom passed the test. Carolyn acted so proud, and he felt stronger than ever. Then his boss urged him to take the government employment test and he did so well, he received a call from the department head at the Internal Revenue Service. He asked Tom to come in for an interview and hired him on the spot. Soon he had blended into the nondescript cast of revenue agents, working long hours, hoping to advance in the job. At least he was assured of regular raises and job security plus the excellent benefits afforded all government workers.

Carolyn loved her job and became a dedicated teacher, patiently working on lesson plans and homework along with a vast array of after school activities. She adored the kids. She directed a play that included children from first to sixth grade, and Tom often joined her at play practice. The children openly flocked to her. Her kindness and gentle ways encouraged them to be the best they could be.

On weekends, they tried to find special time together. They visited the many museums in the Denver area, attended plays at the Denver Center for Performing Arts and had season tickets to the symphony. They were approaching thirty years of age when they decided the time was right to start planning a family. Tom felt the pressure of buying a home and facing a monthly mortgage payment. A child would mean a lot of expense that right now, he just couldn't afford, especially if Carolyn decided to stay at home indefinitely. She looked so happy when they talked about a baby that he knew he had to get ahead, so he could provide a good life for his family.

"Don't worry, Carolyn, we'll make it somehow," he said, kissing her forehead tenderly. She smiled gratefully and cuddled up close to him.

Two Pink Lines

The day it all happened, Wafer left for the office more determined than ever to succeed. He had some tough cases, some that would not respond to his calls at all. But he knew if he could get face to face with a few of them, he just might have some luck. And then the future might look a little better. The great thing about the government was the assured advancement even if you didn't work hard, but if you did, you really got noticed. He had kind of brown-nosed his boss anyway and scored some points that way, but he still needed to do something big.

When Tom arrived at the office that day, a day that changed everything, he turned on his computer and pulled up his calendar. "Call Robert Truax." He clicked "Open File" and looked at the long list of unreturned calls from this Truax fellow. He had been trying to contact him by phone and by mail for more than a year. In fact, another automatically generated letter had gone out just two days ago. This guy owed the government $32,468 including penalties and interest to date. That was a lot of money.

Tom felt a duty to his country to collect that money. It just might be the big hit he needed to push himself up the ladder. His supervisors could not ignore a collection of this amount. Tom re-read the file and saw that the IRS had confiscated his business and equipment. Truax lived in the Long Bow area. Tom clicked on Jefferson County map from his book-marked websites and pulled up Truax's address. It indicated he still owned the mountain property in Long Bow, which meant he had assets.

Tom glanced at his watch and decided there was no time like the present for a field visit. He did a Mapquest search and printed out the map. Those mountain roads were a maze. Grabbing his jacket, he slid the file into his briefcase. Stopping at the reception desk, he let Miriam know he would be out of the office for a while. He said he would check in with her later, but had his pager with him.

***

As soon as Tom left home that morning, Carolyn hurried into the bathroom. She needed to pee so badly she could hardly stand it, but wanted to do the test with her first morning urine, even though the instructions said it need not be. Opening the kit, she took out the test stick and ripped away the foil pouch. On the toilet, she let go a stream, groaning as the flow started. She held the stick in the stream for the required ten seconds and laid it on a paper towel. The instructions said that after about 5 minutes, the small, oval "End of Test" window would turn red, indicating the test was complete. Two pink lines in the window would mean a positive result and possible pregnancy. One pink line would show she was not pregnant. Now she just had to wait five minutes—an interminable length of time. She paced the room, glancing at the clock every minute. Then, she went and looked at the stick—two pink lines had appeared.

A Flash of Hope

B obby heard the phone ring and saw by the caller ID, it was Sandy. His heart jumped, and he grabbed the phone on the second ring.

"Hey baby, what's going on?"

"Not much. I was just thinking about us."

"Yeah, what about us?" Bobby crossed his fingers.

"I don't know. I just wonder where we're going. You know I still love you, but I don't know if I could ever live up there again after all that's happened."

"We don't have to live up here. We could buy a little place somewhere on the outskirts of Denver."

"Would you really leave the mountains?"

"For you, baby, I would. I love you, and I want us to be together again."

Sandy sighed. It was all so complicated, and she wondered if Bobby was really willing to do what it would take.

"Well, I've gotta go. I'll think about it. I love you."

"I love you, too, Babe." He hung up the phone and rubbed his bald head.

No Trespassing!

Tom Wafer headed up Highway 285 toward Long Bow, urging his tiny Ford Escort to keep up with traffic. In Aspen Park, he stopped, gassed up and took another look at his map. Wasn't too far now. Climbing behind the wheel, he headed out, looking for the turn toward the Truax property. After about 3-1/2 miles, he saw the sign and knew he was almost there. Turning down a dirt road marked with all kinds of "Keep Out" signs, he stopped at a beat-up gate. It was a risk to climb over—it was definitely trespassing—it was even marked with a sign, but his goal was too close to be abandoned for a locked gate. Tossing his notebook over, he stuck the toe of his loafer into the chain link, hoisting himself over. Then, dusting his hands, he picked up the notebook and headed down the road toward the Truax place. He admired the beauty of the landscape and thought maybe he and Carolyn might want to live in the hills someday. After a quarter of a mile or so, he heard dogs bark. His pulse quickened.

Making Do

T he morning that everything happened, Bobby had
gone into town like he did every few days to pick
up a few groceries, replenish his liquor supply and get
dog food and other necessities, according to receipts and
mail they found later. He stopped at the mailbox and
turned down his road. He locked the gate and went down
to the house. Mountain folks lock their gates since they
are mostly up there to avoid other people.

They're a strange lot, mountain folks are. They knock
themselves out if you ever ask for help, especially if
it involves their land or yours and anybody trying to
encroach upon, confiscate, or otherwise trespass upon it.
Course, you've got to realize that everybody other than
mountain folks think the land is one big national forest
lying there waiting for them to traipse all over it with
their fancy mountain bikes and backpacks and high-tech
hiking gear. But, other than that, mountain folks would
just as soon stick to themselves and rarely give you the
time of day, except for a passing wave on the road or a
quick conversation at the post office.

So, Bobby arrived home that day and made a couple
of trips out to the truck to unload the groceries. He
unpacked the bag of potato chips and munched a few

handfuls as he put away his groceries in the little pantry off the kitchen. He rubbed his hands together afterward and wiped them on his jeans. Tossing a few small logs into the fireplace to take the chill off the air, he wandered over to the table where he started sorting through his mail, pitching the junk mail into the fire, piece by piece. He came across another bill from the IRS. Goddamn piece of shit IRS, leave me the fuck alone! Haven't they gotten enough, gotten all there is to get? Fuck them, I'll die before I pay them another dime. Fuckers.

This letter, nastier than the last, he threw in the fire, too, like the rest of the notices he had received. But first, he tore it in half, then half again, then into tiny pieces, grinding his teeth as he did. He'd quit paying taxes after they'd closed up his business and didn't report the income from his few odd jobs here and there.

After taking online classes, Bobby became proficient at designing websites and repairing computers. He had his own minor cottage industry going with a simple ad in the local paper. He built up a decent customer base. Best thing, he seldom met with his customers, completing the work via the phone or email and the Internet, which suited him fine. Occasionally, he had to visit someone's home to fix their computer, but he often walked them through the steps by phone or online. People were so grateful that he had little trouble collecting. And even if he did, once Bobby showed up on their doorstep, and they met face to face, they generally paid up right quick. The timing had been perfect with the Internet coming into full bloom soon after his construction business folded.

Life had sure gotten easier since the Internet. Bobby usually had his customers use a money order, so he didn't have to deposit the check into his account plus he'd found some systems like PayPal that handled the payments for you, sending payments directly to a bank account or by check. 'Course, he didn't like banks much either. The IRS could get to funds too easily with a bank account, and they had already levied his. So, he had taken to keeping cash in a small safe he'd built into the wall with a picture hung over it for concealment.

Between the extra income and his VA disability income, which wasn't nearly enough, he managed to get by. He was still twelve years away from social security. To say he lived frugally was an understatement. +-

+He had the place free and clear, used well water, heated with fire and the phone and electricity were about the only things he really needed to run all his computers and satellite dishes, of which he had quite a few. He even grew his own pot in the backyard long before it was legalized in Colorado and to hear tell, it was pretty mean stuff.

The Internet had come in handy for researching UFO's and extraterrestrials, too. Bobby felt encouraged at the talk that the Interplanetary Council might invite planet Earth to join their league. He wasn't sure how they got this type of information, but there were people in contact with ETs. He knew that for sure and hoped he might be one of them someday. He doubted this news as Planet Earth had not yet been invited what with the constant warring that goes on all over the globe. Plus, Bobby knew that there would be a lot of resistance to the idea by people fearful of what it meant, but he had high hopes that, with time, folks would come to accept it. He looked forward to space travel, if he lived long enough. Meantime, he just kept up his own efforts to make contact with aliens.

Bobby made himself a can of Chunky Campbell's soup and sat down with some soda crackers and a beer to read the paper. Sometimes he didn't know why he even read the paper- so much bullshit and lies - and the idiots! He could not believe the stupidity of most people, the things they did for thrills like climbing straight up a rock wall without a rope or bungee jumping - people just begging to die. Well, he didn't have much sympathy for those folks.

After all, he had lived through the real thrill of staying alive in the Nam and the horror of watching real heroes die. He couldn't believe guys like the one who had gone off alone, into the desert, no cell phone, nothing, then he's a hero for cutting off his own arm when he gets stuck. Hero, I'll give you a hero. The guys in Nam who lost arms to save their comrades, threw themselves on a grenade, took the full blow of a Claymore so their buddies could live. Walking the point. Those were the heroes, not these homegrown Rambos, uh-uh.

As he read, he kept the TV on without sound in case something interesting happened. He was getting a little sleepy and beginning to think a nap might sound good when he heard the dogs go nuts. He pushed out from the table sticking one last cracker into his mouth and went to the front porch, which had windows all the way around and a view of the road. He figured it for a deer or elk or one of the other mountain critters, which were in abundance.

Very few people ventured down his road – even the trespassers usually hiked down the creek - and if they did, they were often lost or stupid. It took a lot of audacity to jump a gate covered with signs like "No Trespassing – Violators will be Prosecuted, Guard Dog on Duty", but you'd be surprised how many people ignored such signs. If they could find a way around a locked gate by going off into the woods a short ways to where there's no fence, lots of folks would do it in a heartbeat. They had no respect for private property, or privacy, for that matter.

An Unwanted Visitor

The dogs kept up their frenzied barking, so Bobby knew sure enough they weren't barking at an animal and stood watching. He hung back in the shadows of the room and waited. And damnit if pretty soon he didn't see some guy come around the bend on foot with a notebook under his arm. The dogs really went nuts. The guy didn't look too dangerous. He was small and dressed in a light tan zip up jacket and gray dress pants. He wore a necktie and sported a super-short haircut, the kind you could towel dry—an ordinary fellow.

In fact, it came out later that he was only 30 years old. When they finally found him, a credit card receipt showed he gassed up at the Loaf n' Jug in town before he turned off toward Bobby's place. The attendant remembered him. Least that's what she said later when those newspaper folks converged on her store. Bobby watched from the side front window as the stranger neared the house. He sauntered confidently, gazing around at the mountainside. He heard the barking, so about the time he saw the dogs coming at him, he knelt down, and they turned into mush, wagging their tails and licking him all over. Must've had a way with animals, Bobby guessed. He certainly had little fear of them, anyway. With that, Bobby opened the window a crack and yelled, "Get off this property! You're on private property, go or I'll call the Sheriff!"

"Sir, Mr. Truax, my name is Tom Wafer, I'm a revenue agent with the Internal Revenue Service. I need to talk to you regarding your back taxes."

Well, hearing that just set Bobby off all the more.

"Get the fuck off this property!" he screamed.

Seems this fella fancied himself the Rambo of revenue agents because he wouldn't let up, no matter what Bobby said. By now, Bobby had grown beet red and had worked himself into a rage, calling the agent every name in the book.

"Get the fuck outta here, you dick brain. Don't you understand English? Get! Go! Beat it, you little faggot!"

"Sir, calm down, please. I only need a few moments of your time. This is an important matter. You owe this to your country. Be a patriot and let me in."

That did it! Don't talk to ME about patriotism, you little asshole, Bobby thought.

"Well, you little motherfucker. You don't know shit about being a patriot! Now, get the fuck off his property before you don't have a choice."

The agent kept on coming.

Bobby seethed, and foam bubbled in the corners of his mouth. He dripped with sweat, and the veins in his forehead bulged. The agent had no way of knowing just how much Bobby hated the IRS or how much he prided himself on having served his country in Vietnam. He just kept inching closer to the house until he came around the back corner and ran smack dab into the barrel of Bobby's shotgun. Their eyes met momentarily, and Bobby saw the agent visibly shrink. But then, he sort of raised his shoulders and continued his harangue, like a master negotiator or something.

Don't do it, you dumb shit, don't even think about it. Bobby cocked the shotgun. None of it would have happened if the idiot had just backed off and walked away.

Last Seen

Later on, the news aired an interview with the gal from the Loaf 'n Jug, a tiny thing, who wore a little cap with the store's logo on her bleached-out hair. She was absent her eyetooth on the left side, and she tried to cover it by pulling her top lip down a bit when she talked, giving her the look of someone who'd had a mild stroke.

"Yeah, he came in here that day," she told the television reporter, chewing the cuticle on her right index finger. "I remember him because he took a long time out by the pumps cleaning his windows and headlights and mirrors. He had one of those little Escorts, so I thought it kind of funny that he took such good care of a nothin' little car like that. I mean, we get people in here driving fancy cars, and a lot of them don't take that much time. Anyways, then he came on in to pay and bought a pack of gum and a Big K soda and went on his way. He was friendly and seemed like a nice guy, and I felt bad when I heard what happened." She paused and then asked, "Is this going to be on TV?" She used the flat of her palm and patted the mass of blond thicket that poked out from beneath the little cap. She wished she'd put on some extra lipstick for the event.

Power Trip

Deputy Jason Parks pulled into the Station garage at the end of his shift. He plopped his Sheriff's hat on his head and got out of his patrol car carrying his clipboard and paperwork. He still had an hour or so of work to catch up on. Currently, he worked the three to eleven shift, and that suited him fine because it gave him time in the afternoons to coach grade school soccer. Jason hadn't married yet, though he hoped to, once he found the right woman. He volunteered to coach in one of the soccer leagues that had popped up all over town. He had a great bunch of kids this year with lots of divorced moms who faithfully attended all the games. It was a target rich environment.

Jason had been on the force for five years. After his discharge from the Marines, he entered the police academy. Accustomed to the discipline of military life, he wanted to make it an ongoing part of his own life. He fought in the Gulf War, pushing that bastard Saddam all the way back to Baghdad, but so far as a cop, he'd never unholstered his firearm while on duty. Though he didn't stand out much in a crowd, he managed to hold his own pretty well when a situation called for it.

He worked Jefferson County, which ran from the west suburbs all the way over the Dakota hogback and 15 miles further into the mountains. The west suburbs could be tough as any. Murders, drug arrests, domestic abuse, but the mountain area remained pretty quiet - a nice territory where not much happened aside from an occasional poaching charge or kids vandalizing an empty cabin. Oh, there'd been a bank robbery or two and some neighborhood disputes that got pretty scary and some even ended in murder, but he usually arrived after the action had stopped and helped in the investigation and paperwork.

When the Columbine High School Massacre occurred, he pulled up just as the last shots shattered in the quiet morning air. He had climbed from the cruiser with his shotgun loaded and crouched low around the side of the trunk to retrieve his body armor. He popped the lid and pulled the heavy vest out of the bag, slipping it over his arms. The SWAT team converged on the building, running from tree to tree for cover.

A boy lay in a crumpled heap on the walkway. Poor kid, he lay there all night. His family came about midnight demanding the body of their son, but the decision came down he couldn't be released yet. Bad mistake. The investigation of how the police handled the debacle continued, probably always would. Tremendous blame fell on the Sheriff's Department, maybe justified, maybe not, but a lot of smears on the department and many policy changes. He had to be more careful nowadays, now that the public's eye watched their every move.

Other than a few incidents like that, it was a pretty quiet job, but it gave him authority that he relished. Power. That was the lure, really, power. People Power, Black Power. No - police power, where the power really lay, and he liked it, just as he liked wearing a uniform and packing a gun. Besides, it helped him with the chicks. The only bad part was the solo patrol. He would have liked a partner to ride with; it would at least assuage the boredom that sometimes plagued the solo cop.

Jack Ruffien was on his way to the police garage at the end of his shift. He spotted Jason. Jack, twenty years Jason's senior, felt like a kid himself. He often thought the great thing about getting older was just your body got older. Your mind and spirit gelled in your twenties when you liked yourself and felt good about life. Then you just stayed the same all the rest of your life, except you got quite a bit smarter as time went on and used the big head a lot more often than the little head.

Not that it had been easy. Jack had been a hell raiser most of his early life. He'd always said if he hadn't been a cop, he'd have probably been in jail, which wasn't all that uncommon for the type of guys on the department. Most of them just needed a place to channel all that testosterone. Law enforcement gave them a legal way to kick ass and intimidate people and most of the guys loved that aspect of it. But Jack, with only three years left until retirement, looked forward to time on the links and traveling with his wife. God knew Joleen looked forward to his retirement. She worried every time he walked out the door in his uniform. He picked up his cell phone and speed dialed her number.

"Hey, babe, it's me. What're you doing? Yeah, I'm just heading for the barn, running a little late—too many speeders out there today. I'll be home in a while. You need anything? Okay, I love you, too. Hey, let's go out for dinner tonight. Bye."

Joleen was a great wife and mother. Hell, she'd managed to get those two boys educated and married to good girls, and he knew she had a lot more to do with all that than he ever did given the weird hours he'd worked most of his career. She just had way of gentle coercion that kept them all, including him, on the straight and narrow.

The boys had never given them any major cause for worry about drugs or been the kind of thugs Jack and his buddies had been at their ages. Oh, Tommy had had his struggle with grades and Ricky had been a bit of a partier, booze and all, but nothing major. Now they both had good jobs in the computer/telecom industry and were making the big bucks. Tommy's wife Susan was pregnant, and he would soon be a grandpa. They already knew it was a girl and planned to name her Jacqueline after him. He was a lucky man, and he knew it. The seve—to-three shift ended.

TWITCHY FINGER

B obby held the shotgun steady, staring into the revenue agent's eyes.

"Now, Mr. Truax, we can work this entire issue out peaceably. Please put your gun down. You do not have to be a hero. This is just a tax bill," he implored, holding up one palm and moving toward Bobby.

Well, that did it. Bobby's finger twitched once, then pulled on the trigger and pret' near blew the guy's head right off. Bobby was almost as surprised as the agent, who exploded backward into a dead, bloody heap. He stepped back and stood looking a bit puzzled, his hands shaking. He lowered the gun, setting the butt on the ground as he scratched his chin and took a few steps backward. Lucky for Bobby, most of the blood and spray of bits of bones and gray matter blew away from the house and didn't make too much of a mess.

Blood poured out into the tall grass and had sprayed all over the bushes and yard. The dogs had run behind the garage when they spotted his shotgun, but had cautiously returned, drawn by the smell of blood and were now sniffing around and lapping up the puddle like it was honey.

The guy lay in pieces and Bobby stood over him for a minute, trying to figure out what happened. He leaned the gun against the house as he pulled off his ball cap and scratched his head with the same hand, looking around the mountain to make sure nobody came with this guy. The mountain lay quiet save for the sharp call of a magpie and the gentle chirping of birds, which had resumed their song soon after the loud blast of the shotgun. All he could see were the quaking aspens, their leaves rustling in the wind and the deep green pine forest beyond. He scanned the grassy hillsides for movement and saw none. The revenue agent seemed to be alone, and Bobby took a minute to catch his breath and think things over.

FLY ME TO THE MOON

Bobby stood over the mangled corpse in his blood-stained clothes and knew he had a big problem on his hands. Flashing on his life and the man he was, he knew at that moment that he could not go to jail. Without a doubt, he could never put up with the confinement of prison or the assholes that filled them. Scanning the isolated mountainside again, he decided he had to get rid of the headless corpse somehow. Feeling the guy's front pants pockets, he found a lump.

Stretching open the right pocket with one hand, he pushed two fingers down inside and got a hold of Wafer's car keys and slid them out. Rolling him over, he found his wallet and the pager and took those, too. Flipping open the wallet, he saw the guy's name—Thomas Wafer—age 30, who lived down in the Denver area. He closed the wallet, taking it and the pager along with his gun into the kitchen and laying them on the table. Digging around in the cabinet under the sink, he found some black trash bags, which he took outside and spread open on the ground.

"Go on, you mutts, get outta here!" he yelled, shooing the dogs away again and leaning down, trying to keep his already spattered boots out of the puddling blood. He squatted over the body and folded the legs up toward where its head used to be and bent the body somewhat in half. A live body felt heavy, but a dead one was near impossible to manage. He sweated and panted as he struggled mightily to stuff Wafer's 145-pounds, which now seemed like two hundred, into one bag. Then he looked around and ran his hands through the tall grass, looking for any chunks of bone and cooling flesh he could find that were big enough to pick up. He set the severed arm on top of the body.

Bobby had been a hunter for years, so handling a warm, dead creature was nothing new to him, not to mention what he had to do just to get through Vietnam. He gathered up all the pieces and tossed them into the sack. After he wrapped the whole mess up good and tight, he rolled it all into a second bag and then tied some nylon rope around it to keep it together. Grabbing the bag by the ropes, he lugged it over and set it near the driveway while he spread a piece of Visqueen on the concrete apron in front of the garage and hoisted the bag onto it. Turning on the hose, he began spraying down the entire area to get rid of all the blood and gore. Bits and chunks were clinging to rocks and blades of grass as the blood congealed.

From watching all those forensic shows, he knew all about luminal, the chemical that can detect bloodstains, even years later, but kept his fingers crossed, it would never come to that. By now, the Goddamn dogs' faces and paws were covered in blood, too, so he had to hose them down. They hated the hose and ran behind the garage to hide, but he caught them and held them by the scruffs of their necks and rubbed their fur and faces until the blood disappeared.

He hosed off the side of the house where some of the gore hung in tiny chunks and droplets, putting off a terrible stench. That smell of water and blood turned his stomach. It reminded him of when he worked at the chicken processing plant during high school. His job required him to wait until the chickens came by, hung upside down on the conveyer line. He was to cut their throats with an electric knife as they went by. He never got over the smell of blood on ice, even though he only lasted three days at the job. He remembered the old ladies there laughing at him, at his weak stomach and his revulsion. Most of them had worked there for years and took it all in stride.

With a farmer blow, he headed toward the garage to find some tools. He scrounged around, cursing the disorder until he found a shovel and rake. He laid them over his shoulder and walked down to the road beside the scene of the crime. Scooping up a couple of shovels full of sand and dirt from the road, he spread it over the area to mask the smell and raked and hosed it down a bit more. Standing back for an objective view, he thought it looked pretty good, pretty normal.

He looked up at the sky and saw the sun shining down from almost directly above. Inside the house, he took off his bloody shirt and jeans before he lathered up his hands and arms and washed up pretty well. Splashing cold water on his freshly scrubbed face, he contemplated his options, and knew he didn't have many. Dousing the bloody clothes with paint thinner, he threw them in the fire and poked it all around real good until it caught. Then did the same with his own boots, which he sorely hated to lose because they were his best work boots, and they weren't cheap with the lift and all. He couldn't afford to have anything bloody around if he could help it. He changed into a clean T-shirt and jeans and shoved his feet into an old pair of boots.

Then he drove to the gate and opened it, getting into the Escort, which sat parked off to the side of the road. He looked around, hoping no one had driven by and spotted the car. He drove it back to the house, pulling it up near the body. Then he walked back to get his pickup. He carried a broom to sweep away the tire marks along the entire length of the road, which spanned a good quarter mile. Finally, pulling a rag from his pocket, he wiped the gate free of all the fingerprints from Wafer climbing over it and locked it up. He thought he was pretty thorough.

When he got back to the house, he backed up and picked up the body, which, given the size of the guy, felt a lot heavier than Bobby had thought it should be. He loaded it in the back of his pickup and tossed in a shovel and pick. His back was killing him, and he stretched and groaned. He knew he had some heavy work ahead, so he went inside and grabbed his little igloo cooler, throwing in some ice with a couple of beers. He poked around in the fridge and found some stuff to make a tuna fish salad sandwich, which he ate standing over the sink to catch any crumbs or drips. Rinsing his hands, he grabbed the cooler and a bottle of water and loaded up. He drove off into the backwoods with the dogs in the rear bed with the body.

Now you've got to understand, we're talking about a thousand acres or more at the end of a box canyon that encompasses several landowners' properties, but most of them were just vacant parcels. Bobby had hiked and hunted and driven it for years and knew it like the back of his hand. He was sure there were plenty of canyons and ravines in which to hide the body and really no way for anybody to spot a fresh grave. He would have just driven the damn Escort if he didn't need to put the truck in 4-wheel drive to get up hills and through the soft dirt between the trees.

There was silence save the sound of the wheels crawling over rocks and holes and berry bushes and the trees scraping the side of the truck as he broke a trail. He got way back, deep into the woods and found a wide ravine. He could drive down in far enough to find a well-concealed spot. Emerging from the truck, he started walking around a bit, jabbing in here and there with the shovel. He found a good soft area that was mostly washed down topsoil, and the digging was pretty easy. It was an area where nobody had been in years, if ever. Backing the truck out, he turned around and backed into the ravine, so the bed pointed toward the place where he planned to dig. He stood staring into the dense grove of dark timber, pondering his predicament and wondering how things had gotten to this point. He began to dig.

Dead. Dammit. Dead. He's dead, more dead, deader than dead, Bobby, thought. Goddamn IRS, *taxman, taxman gonna getcha, gotta getcha, taxman, here comes the taxman, here come the judge, here come the judge. Judge, judge, judge, jury and executioner. Hangman, pick a letter, name the phrase, name the game, name of the game. The name game. Bobby bobby bo bobby, Bobby's mind wandered as he dug. If the first two letters are ever the same, drop them both and say the name....*

The ground gave way beneath his shovel like sand on a wet beach. It chunked off the end of the spade and disintegrated when it hit the grass beside the hole. Chunk, crack, he hit a rock. Fuck, he thought. No wonder nothing grows out here but grass and trees. Rocks, that's why they call 'em the Rocky Mountains, never seen so many rocks. He dug and dug, hitting the rock over and over, breaking the thin granite into shattered slabs, kneeling down now and then to pull out a rock too big to break. The impact of the shovel against the rock reverberated up his arms and into his shoulders and back, over and over again.

Chunk, chunk. The silence broke only by the steady sound of the shovel striking the dense rocky earth and the chatter of a squirrel high up in the trees above, warning them away from its nest. Protective bastard. Just like me, on the defense, no defense like a good offense. He kept up at a steady pace for an hour or so, only using the pick a couple of times when he had to get the big rocks out.

Hell, he'd done this every day of his life in Vietnam. His mind drifted back to those days of heat and wet and bugs and dirt. He remembered the first foxhole he ever dug and how interminable the process had seemed though he was in a helluva lot better shape back then. Digging, dig it, dig it man, dig that hole, push that barge, pull that train, train wreck, that was his life — a train wreck. Turn that train around, turn around, no turning back, man, no turning back now. Back now, backhoe, wish I had backhoe, could really use a backhoe now.

He kept on digging, stopping occasionally to wipe the sweat off his face with the sleeve of his t-shirt and to catch his breath while he gulped the cool water. The ache was beginning to set into his shoulders, but he shrugged it off, there no time for that, no time left, *no time left for you, no time left for you. Oooh, yeah, yeah, yeah, yeah,* thought Bobby. *Wish I could, I'd fly my ass to the moon, fly me to the moon and let me play among the stars. Yeah, Mars, if only one of those alien spacecrafts would fly me to the moon....*

A Simple Burial

The dogs always thought backwoods jaunts were great fun and ran around chasing squirrels and rabbits. After sniffing under logs for a while, they lay under the shady trees. Now, they watched him dig. It took him a couple of hours altogether, and he dug that hole a good four feet deep and three feet wide. By then, he felt tired and thirsty and grateful for having the foresight to bring along the beer. When he got the hole big enough, he dusted himself off, sat on the tailgate, and swigged a cold one, relishing the burning, bubbly sensation in his throat. Pushing off, he forced himself to keep going. He still had a lot of work to do.

Backing the truck up as close as he could without taking a chance on getting stuck, he positioned it so he wouldn't have to haul the body too far. He shut off the engine, climbed out, and slid the bundle onto the tailgate. Hoisting it off, he let it drop to the ground. Then he rolled it over twice and dumped it into the hole where he sat on the edge and rested, looking up at the clear, bluebird sky.

The cool, fresh earth was black, and Bobby grabbed a handful and held it up to his nose. It smelled rich and fertile, and he thought it would be great garden soil. Rains always drove the topsoil down into the ravines where the aspens and wildflowers flourished. The late summer sun cast an amber glow and the high clouds formed a halo around Pike's Peak. The afternoon temperature stayed high, but he knew he was running out of daylight with all he had left to do. He finished his beer and forced himself to his feet. Grabbing the shovel, he dumped dirt on the body, watching the black lump disappear beneath the shovels full of dirt he tossed into the maddeningly slow-to-fill hole. He buried the body in less time than it had taken to dig the hole.

When he finished shoveling, he smoothed the dirt with the rake and then covered it with leaves and branches and pine needles, which camouflaged it pretty well from what the Sheriff told the reporters later. Then he threw the tools in the back with a clunk, barely missing the waiting dogs and popped the second beer. He drank it down in a few swigs on his way back to the house and wondered how he had gotten into this mess. He thought about his life and how different it had turned out than he planned. Thinking about little Bobby and Sandy, he flashed on how beautiful she looked holding the baby the day he was born.

A slight smile crept across his mouth until his thoughts wandered to the day little Bobby died. It was an image he tried to bury in his memory, but now and then, it rushed back with a vengeance. He could picture Bobby lying on the cold concrete of the garage floor, blood pooling around his small body and him dropping to his knees in abject agony at the sight. He blinked back a tear and turned onto his road, shaking off the image as best he could, forcing himself back to the present, to the nightmare he had created once again.

After he washed the shovel and pick and the tires of the pickup, he hid the tools in the garage. There wasn't much he could do about the tires tracks he'd left driving through the brush and woods. He'd just have to cross his fingers on that part. The dry weeds would hold the impression of the tire marks for weeks or at least until the next good rain, which looked to be a ways off, judging by the weather reports, whatever good they were.

FINAL STEP

B obby swept the driveway and went into the house to wash the sweat and grime off his hands and face. Exhausted, he stood at the kitchen sink and let the water flow until ice cold water filled his glass. It was one of the best things about mountain living—the ice-cold well water—so much sweeter and purer than chemically tainted city water. Then he bent forward and splashed the soothing water over his face again and again. Turning to the fridge, he popped another beer. It, too, was ice cold and bubbled down his dry throat, soothing his body and calming his brain. This one he sipped while he flipped on the tube. He dropped in a weary heap at the table and poured a shot of Jack. Since he still had to deal with the car and was running on empty, he needed all the help he could get .

Absently munching on a bag of chips, he stared off into space with a look like the legendary thousand-yard stare. He'd experienced it firsthand in Nam, but every war had produced it. The dead look in the eyes of those soldiers who had seen it all and no longer felt a thing. Turning back to the news, he shook his head. God, he'd be glad when this election season ended. He couldn't take much more of those goofballs and the endless debates!

Bobby conjured up his remaining energy and headed out to the garage. Scrounging around, he found a length of hose. He opened the Escort's gas cap and stuck the hose in and sucked hard, spitting as the foul liquid reached his mouth. He siphoned most of the gas out of the Escort into a couple of gas cans, so the car wouldn't catch fire when he dumped it. The tank was so full, it seemed like it would never empty, but he was grateful this Wafer fellow was the type to drive such a little piece of shit vehicle, one that would be easy to hide. He just hoped it would handle driving through the hills. He glanced around the mountain, watching the occasional yellow aspen leaf flutter to the ground on a wisp of wind.

A magpie squawked as the dog darted toward it till it flew up onto the branch of a tall pine. He wished he had wings to fly away. Grabbing a landscape saw, some rope, and an old green canvas tarp he had stored in the rafters of the garage, he stuffed the whole mess in the trunk, squeezing his massive body behind the wheel with a groan. Turning the Escort around, he drove way back into the woods again, this time in a different direction. The little four-banger strained to climb the hills even in low gear, and he wondered what possessed Coloradoans to own such little wimpy vehicles. Oh well, at least it was an American car instead of one of those junk rice burners.

He glanced at his watch. Three-thirty. This time he headed toward the lip of the canyon, deep into the forest on an old, rarely-used logging road, high above an uninhabited area where you could see for miles. He forced the little car over fallen limbs, weaving through dense overgrown gooseberry and currant bushes whose few remaining berries had dried up with the first hard frost. He tried picking those damn things a few times with Sandy. She liked to make jam, and it was damn good at that, but what a pain to pick. Every branch bore fine thorns that poked and stuck their tips into the skin of his finger, tough as they were. And the berries, tiny, little pea size things with a stem on one end and the dried flower on the other, both of which had to be picked off before cooking. It meant sorting through and handling every berry individually. Seemed like too much trouble to Bobby. But he'd learned not to argue about some things—to pick his battles. Well, he'd probably picked the wrong battle this time. Yep, he had a real bad feeling about this battle.

The little car struggled along through the underbrush that had long since overtaken parts of the path, bumping and dodging, crunching over decayed logs. A couple of times, he held his breath as the little car strained, acting like it wouldn't make it up the hills, but it continued to plug along, and he got through just the same. He inched carefully along the ridge, precariously close to the drop off and drove it right up to the edge of the cliff, where he could see Cathedral Spires and the whole Buffalo Creek forest fire area, now brown and barren with just a few small trees and pale buffalo grass holding it all together.

Those poor people had lived through hell. First, the tremendous forest fire, which took out houses and ranches and cabins. He remembered that day. Standing in his front yard watching that white cloud billow upward until it engulfed the entire sky to the south. As the fire raged, the smoke took on an orange hue and black smoke climbed upward. It burned for days with planes buzzing overhead, dropping the red slurry fire retardant while smoke jumpers fought the hot spots.

When it was all over, some 12,000 acres had burned, and it seemed like he'd heard around 20 homes and cabins went, too. That was all in 1996. Flash flooding resulted in mudslides. Those miserable souls had just about had enough when a local newspaper cartoonist had produced a cartoon in which a meteor careened toward earth. The caption read something like, "The meteor appears to be headed toward a small town in Colorado called Buffalo Creek." You had to laugh.

Bobby put the Escort in park and got out and made sure of what lay below. The cliff angled down on an angle, and tall trees skirted the area. Rough underbrush filled the deep canyon yawning below. He thought it looked just about as good as it could get. So, he reached in the car window, slipped it in neutral and just pushed it real easily over the edge. It started slowly, rolled over in midair and then fell about 30 feet with a tremendous crash, landing on its nose, but it didn't catch fire even though it tore through quite a few tree limbs. It came to rest wedged between a very tall lodgepole pine and the rock wall itself, nestled well into the thick, dark underbrush.

Deep Shit

B obby tossed down the rope and canvas tarp with the hand saw inside it, and both landed near the car with a thud. Perched on the edge of the cliff, he searched until he found a foothold and then eased himself around and began the slow, circuitous climb down the thirty feet of slanted rocks. With terrain rugged enough, he could step from ledge to crevasse as he made his way down with rocks crumbling and breaking away as he descended. He climbed on down the canyon wall, and when he got to the car, he leaned against it, panting, while he rested for a minute or two to catch his breath. His breathing slowed, and he pulled up the front of his t-shirt and wiped his sweaty, dirty face.

Running on fumes himself, he sighed with relief to be nearly done. He grabbed the tarp, lapping it twice like a bed sheet to cover the Escort so it wouldn't shine in the sun or be too easy to spot if anyone flying over or hiking in the distance. Many a time, he had spotted an otherwise obscured house on the mountainside when the rays of the sun hit its windows just right. He spread it over the car, stuffing it down through the brush with a long stick, pulling it around as best he could. With a lot of lower branches he'd cut from the trees along with some of the broken ones, he covered the car with a good, heavy layer.

To finish, he put some big rocks on top of everything to hold it all in place and tied it all up real well like a big old package, kneeling down on the rocky surface and wrapping the rope under and around the wheels and over the hood. The difficult footing made him slip on the loose rocks a few times before he leaned back and looked it over. He believed he'd hidden it just about as good as he possibly could.

The ascent seemed a little easier than climbing down, and he slipped the curved handle of the saw over his shoulder as he went. He slowly inched his way to the top, fearful of looking back down. He pushed himself up and over but faltered once on top, almost losing his footing and stumbling backward, but he caught onto a bush and steadied himself, heart pounding in his ears and adrenalin pulsing in his veins as he clung to the edge of the cliff.

"Jesus Christ! I 'bout killed myself," he cursed his lament. He talked out loud to himself now, half nuts from the whole thing. He walked back and forth along the ledge a few times, checking whether his camouflage had worked. It looked pretty good, and he thought he had a plan. It all seemed like the only way to go.

Now he had no vehicle, so he started hoofing it on back to the house in the growing darkness, careful where he walked. His leg ached, and he forced himself onward through the rough terrain. The sun had lowered, and the amber glow had faded to a pinkish blush across the sky with a few wispy clouds floating against the deepening blue background. He could see Pike's Peak and thought it wouldn't be long before the summit would be dressed in white with the canyon blanketed in deep camouflaging snow covering the damn car better yet. He prayed this would be one of those years of heavy snowfall that didn't quit until May, keeping the car well buried.

He limped along, stepping over fallen timber and climbing between the lower branches that blocked his path, stumbling on rocks and occasionally catching the toe of his boot on a hidden branch. Mountain hiking is tough under the best of circumstances, but as you can imagine with his age and the limp and all, not to mention the adrenalin rush that had long since faded, he was pretty whipped.

He saw the house in the distance and the dogs ran up to meet him, tails wagging like he'd been gone for days. Simple life they had. Sometimes he wished he could just be a dog. He stopped to pet them both and dumped some food in their bowl. He opened the back door and went straight to the sink where he opened the faucet until the water ran good and cold, and he filled a tall glass. He drank it straight down and had half a glass more.

You'd think a Goddamn Vietnam vet would have sense enough to pack water on a venture like this. He shook his head at his own stupidity and walked into the living room carrying a bag of taco chips and beer. Too tired to cook, he mindlessly ate the chips and washed them down with the cold beer. He sighed and groaned as the ache grew and inundated his entire body right down to the bone. Then, he stretched, tossed back a double shot of whiskey and laid down on the quilt that covered his bed, dirt and all, sleeping straight through the night.

Whup, whup, whup. He woke with a start the next day, sweating and dreaming of Vietnam medevacs and headless corpses, and that's when he came to the stark and terrible realization that he was probably in some really deep shit.

A Bad Feeling

C arolyn dialed Tom's pager number for the umpteenth time that afternoon. She bit her bottom lip and pondered her unanswered pages. She had a bad feeling. Tom always called her within a half an hour or so of her page. She'd called the office and Miriam, the receptionist, had told her Tom had been out in the field all day and hadn't called in.

"Is that normal, Miriam, for him not to call in before five?"

"Not really, Carolyn, he's pretty good about touching base, but who knows, something may have come up. Don't worry, I'm sure you'll hear from him soon."

Not the least bit reassured by the conversation, Carolyn stirred the Bearnaise sauce she had prepared for the filets and stared off at nothing. Her mind wandered to the baby, their beautiful, perfect little baby, and a tiny smile crept across her lips. Tom would be so thrilled when she told him. She set the spoon down and turned off the heat beneath the sauce, looking at the kitchen clock again.

Six-thirty. So unlike him. She had set the table with fresh flowers she'd picked up at the supermarket and her wedding China, once again admiring the pattern she had chosen. She didn't use it often, and it always reminded her of their wedding day. Tom had looked so handsome in his black tux and white cummerbund, his hair combed to the side. Where could he be, anyway?

She straightened the tablecloth and silverware a bit and walked into the living room, snatching her Gourmet magazine from the pile of mail on the way. She picked up the remote control and popped on the tube, plopping on the sofa. Sukie, their Siamese cat, jumped on the sofa next to her, purring.

"Hi, Sukie, how's the little kitty cat?" Carolyn crooned, stroked the soft, beige fur of the young feline. Sukie had been a first anniversary present from Tom to Carolyn and a treasured member of their little family. Tom had arrived home carrying a basket with a big pink bow and a soft blanket that wriggled when he presented it to her. She peeled back the blanket, and the kitten had let out a distinctly Siamese meow. It was love at first sight.

"Where's your daddy, Sukie? Why isn't he home yet?" Sukie stretched upward, arching her back and rubbing against Carolyn's hand. Then she curled up next to her and fell asleep. Carolyn opened her magazine and leafed through the pages with little interest. She looked up when the clock chimed seven times. Carolyn turned on the table lamp and slid down into a more comfortable position and began reading an article about Parisian coffee. She slept fitfully through the night.

Out of Sight

B obby groaned as he pushed himself up on the edge
of the bed, running a hand over his hairless head.
That old Vietnam dream had not happened in quite a
while, though it had plagued him for years. Whup, whup,
whup. It always woke him with a frightening start. His
back ached and his leg throbbed. He didn't realize he
had allowed himself to fall into such awful shape. He
still wore his dirty clothes and boots. Leaning down,
he unlaced the boots, pushing them off with his toes,
and peeling off the stinking socks. Twisting from side
to side, he rubbed his lower back, stood up and limped
awkwardly toward the kitchen.

Few people realized Bobby had a limp because they
always saw him wearing his special shoe, but without it,
his leg was a good three inches shorter than the other
one. It resulted in a staggering walk, his body pumping
from side to side. As he passed by, he turned up the
volume of the television he'd left on all night and headed
for the kitchen.

"Coffee," he moaned. He half listened to the television
as he put three scoops of coffee in the filter, but he heard
nothing about it on the news, and he breathed what he
knew was a premature sigh of relief.

Given that, he poured his black coffee and sat at the table in front of the big window. He never learned to drink coffee with all the frou-frou creamer shit. Hot and black, just like in the Nam. Opening the little canister where he kept his reefer, he rolled a joint while he considered all his options. He finally decided his best bet was to just sit tight. He'd covered all the bases and felt like he had things pretty well under control.

The revenue agent's wallet sat accusingly in front of him. He picked it up and looked through all the ID's and credit cards one by one and thought the guy looked like a stable sort—he had an American Express Gold Card, anyway. Sifting through the dog-eared photos, he came across a picture of a red-headed girl standing in front of what looked to be some sort of vacation spot, judging by the expansive view in the background. She was wearing shorts and a pink T-shirt while smiling brightly at the camera. He figured she must be his wife, judging by the wedding ring Wafer wore. He felt bad, guilt sticking him like a burr, but there was no turning back now.

The notebook held the file folder with Bobby's social security number on it along with his old tax ID number from the business and contained his whole miserable history with the IRS. He leafed through it, gnashing his teeth and getting pissed off all over again. He saw the tally of how much they had collected from him in all - $173,596.32. This, of course, included the value of all of his equipment from the business, accounts receivable, his vehicles, and his bank accounts. But they still wanted more, Goddamn it, they still wanted more!

Suddenly, Bobby felt justified in his actions and any remorse he'd felt before began to dwindle rapidly. He ripped the pages from the file, wadding them into balls and pitching them into the fireplace on top of the remains of his burned clothes and boots, which now threw off a foul and lingering odor. He tossed in the wallet and squirted paint thinner on all of it and tossed in a match, watching with satisfaction as it burned, gray smoke curling upward, carrying more of the nightmare with it. As it burned down, he stirred up the ashes and threw some newspaper in on top and doused it all again. He went outside and grabbed an armful of small kindling and piled it on top of the evidence.

He showered and stood under the hot spray for twenty minutes until the aches and pains subsided, and he felt almost human again. He leaned forward and let the spray hit his bald head and pondered his future. As he toweled off, he grimaced at the bags he saw under his eyes in the mirror.

After he dressed, he stirred the fire around for a while and checked periodically to see if the ashes had cooled. Finally, digging all the remnants out of the fireplace, he put them in a metal bucket and hurried outside because it still smoked some. Hauling it up the hill, he slung a shovel over his shoulder. He found a spot near the spring where the soft dirt made the digging easy, and buried the smoking ashes along with the beeper, which had gone off numerous times. There was always the same number for call-back. Probably his wife, Bobby thought. Too bad. Too fuckin' bad.

He limped back to the house and rinsed out the bucket and washed the shovel again. Now, came the worst part—the matter of waiting. No telling how efficient those IRS folks actually were—like, did he tell them where he was going and that kind of stuff? Would anybody report him missing? If he weren't married, it would be at least a while before somebody called the cops, so he'd probably have a day or two. But since he was, time was short, if he'd calculated correctly.

Figuring he had at least one day, he started pouring shots of Jack chased with beer and got good and fucked up to dull the fear that lurked in the back of his mind. It was already eleven o'clock when he slept, and he had slept later than usual. Watching for news updates on the tube all day, he fooled around with his computer and answered a few emails. He had a couple of jobs to finish and appointments to make, but that could wait. He was too brain dead to deal with any of it.

Finally, he passed out around five o'clock and slept hard. About midnight, he struggled to regain consciousness. A nagging noise would not let up. It was an incessant barking. His dogs were barking. He rubbed his eyes and pressed his palms against the sides of his pounding head, and then it became clear. He could hear dogs barking wildly in the distance.

Now, mind you, that's not all that uncommon in the mountains given the critters that are out roaming around at night, like mountain lions and elk. In fact, mountain lions had been killing dogs in the hills lately. The big old cats usually waited until they could catch their prey unaware and pounced from behind, snapping their neck in one quick shake. Then they dragged them off to an obscure spot, usually under a big tree or something where they could feast safely. Many a dog owner had found his best buddy buried in a shallow grave of pine needles and snow and dirt, half eaten; the cat planning to return later for another meal.

But the way the dogs were barking sounded a little different to him than when they barked at an animal. It was the sound of fear, all rapid and wild with low, prolonged growls. He sat up on the edge of the bed, rubbed his face, and ran his hand over his bald head. Bracing himself on the side of the bed for a moment before he got up, he finally staggered outside.

The chilly night air hit him hard, tingling his face and bringing goose bumps to his flesh. His breath froze before him, and he hugged himself with both arms. As his head cleared, fear clutched at his throat. He sucked in his breath and listened intently. The dogs drew nearer, and he called out to them. They came running and seemed to be on high alert. They listened, too, standing close and jerking around nervously.

Then he saw the intensely bright lights in the distant sky, and he just knew it was a UFO. The lights were amazingly bright and seemed to hover perfectly still and silent for a moment or two, but then just clean disappeared as though it had never been there at all. He stayed outside for a while before he realized he was shivering from head to toe. He went inside to get his big 80,000 candle power light and laser beam while he pulled on a jacket and chugged a tall glass of cold water. Damn, he had hot pipes.

Outside again, he shined both lights up into the sky for twenty minutes, swinging them back and forth, searching for the object that he had seen, wondering if he had actually seen it at all. Finally, when he was fairly certain that whatever he'd seen was not coming back, he went inside and crawled back into bed. He lay awake for a while, shaking like a leaf and pondering the events of the last couple of days, trying to make some sense of it all, before he fell back into a deep sleep.

Whup, whup, whup. The next morning, he woke at first light with his head still pounding and his parched throat on fire and that damned dream about the Nam and the helicopters. Cursing the half empty bottle of Jack, he went through the morning ritual of building a fire, making coffee and watching the tube a little more closely, waiting with bated breath for the news to hit. He checked his email and fooled around with one website he was building, but couldn't keep his mind on his work. After a while, he drove into town for gas and picked up the newspaper and a sandwich from Subway.

He drove past his turnoff so he could see if there was anyone waiting at his gate when he arrived home, but it was quiet and all clear. After he fed the dogs, he sat down at his table to eat the dripping sandwich while he read the paper cover to cover. He kept an ear to the radio in case they should report it, but there wasn't a damn thing about a missing person anywhere.

He didn't know whether to relax or worry more, so he worked on the website that he needed to complete within the next week. He surfed the net, poking into

UFO sites and sightings, hoping for some confirmation of activity in his area. The phone had not rung in two days, and he figured that was good. No phone calls to track his whereabouts.

Getting Out of Dodge

The days were getting cooler and the house, old as it was, didn't have the best insulation. Originally, there had only been chinked logs, but the first owners had finally broken down and insulated behind the paneling they installed, and that had made it tighter and warmer. The windows were old and leaked like a sieve, and even the storm windows didn't help. He walked out to the woodpile and gathered another big armload of pine. Arranging it in the fireplace, he threw in some newspaper, and got a fire going. He welcomed the warmth and the elimination of any traces of evidence that remained.

The day dragged by, his heart pounding at every sound and news report. He must have looked at the clock a thousand times. That evening, when he was finishing up a can of Dinty Moore Beef Stew, he heard the dogs bark again and looked through the window. Darkness had fallen, and he thought he saw a bright light in the sky again. This time, he had prepared. Dousing the lights, he grabbed his 80,000-candle power lamp and laser beam to scan the sky. There was not a cloud in the sky, and the moon hadn't yet appeared.

He saw the lights, but the object didn't appear to be a plane or a helicopter, so he started signaling again the way they said to do at the institute and, sure enough, the light seemed to get brighter and come closer. His pulse raced as the dogs whined and shinnied up next to him real close. He tried to still his rapid breathing and hold the lights steady.

He made many attempts, but the light hovered above. It came close enough that he could hear the wind from it and feel it against his face. Leaves rustled across the ground, and the dogs' fur ruffled. Then, the UFO just disappeared into thin air. He waited awhile before going inside, chuckling to himself that if there was ever a time for an abduction, this would be that time.

Next afternoon, he was out chopping wood when he heard the phone ring. The ring startled him, and he dropped the axe and headed in to answer, but the machine picked up before he could.

"Mr. Truax, this is Deputy Dilbert from the Jefferson County Sheriff's office. We are investigating a missing person case and need to speak with you. Please call me at your earliest convenience. Thanks." He left the number, which Bobby noted on the edge of the newspaper.

"Shit." Here we go, man. Here we go. Okay, okay, this is no time to panic. He'd been in tougher spots than this in Nam. He had to stay calm, think it through, and get a plan. Plan your work and work your plan. Get out of town. That's it. Get out of town. They had nothing on him. No evidence.

Bobby went out and backed his truck up to the garage where he kept the tent, sleeping bag and cook stove all in one place. He stowed the gear in the truck bed. He tossed in a shovel, too, along with some split firewood into the back of truck. No point in rummaging around in the dark. Half the time, there was no firewood to be found, anyway.

Carrying the cooler into the house to wash it, he loaded it up, replaying the message in his mind. They knew that Wafer fellow had been on his way to Bobby's place. Too Goddamn efficient, these friggin' revenue agents. He mumbled and cursed as he threw some food in the cooler, packed some dry goods and a couple of pots and pans. He waited until dark so he could drive out with his lights off, unnoticed.

The drive out was quiet, and he headed toward the national forest, maintaining the speed limit and keeping an eye on the rearview mirror for the cops. Assholes. Now he had to deal with the assholes again. Never leave me alone, always got to be on my back. That stupid s.o.b. deserved what he got, coming onto my property, demanding money, questioning my patriotism. Goddamn that motherfucker!

He drove along the darkened highway, staying in the right lane, watching the commuter traffic fly by, anxious to get home. As he passed Bailey, the traffic thinned, and he found himself alone on a long stretch of darkened highway. An occasional pair of illuminated eyes caught his attention as he cruised along. He finally hit the huge open flats just past Kenosha Pass and turned north into the mountains. He and Sandy and Bobby had camped back in there before, and he knew a nice, isolated spot where no one could find him. Locating the turnoff he'd used before, he followed the narrow road back as far as he could.

He found the remote spot deep in the forest and eased his truck into the clearing. The remnants of a campfire pit offered easy heat and cooking. Bobby found his Coleman lantern and pumped it up before he lit a stick match and set it aglow. The flame glowed, and he turned it down to a steady light. He hung it on a long, bare branch on the tall pine that towered over the camp spot. He pulled the cooler out of the back of the truck and cracked a cold beer to sip while he worked. Set up the tent first, he had always preached. That way, if you get too fucked up or tired, you've always got a place to drop. Nothing worse than being drunk with no where to crash.

Sandy had been pretty good about that. Made a nice little camp site for them, setting everything up neat and nice. He spread the tent out and popped it up, pounding the stakes into each corner. Pretty nice, the way the tents just about go up by themselves now, he thought. In the old days, he remembered all the poles and ropes and stakes and the heavy canvass that took an hour to put up and arrange. Then he pulled out his cocoon sleeping bag and spread it out on the foam mat inside the tent. No point in freezing his ass off. Might as well be warm.

It got goddamn cold up in the mountains even in the fall, hell, even in the summer. Many a time he had crawled out of the tent on a summer morning and shivered his ass off while he built the fire for breakfast. He thought about the poor GIs freezing to death in the Ardennes forest during the Battle of the Bulge. Man, oh man! No warm clothes, poor equipment, never heard of Gortex back then. Just plain old, lined pants and jacket, huddled together in the foxholes for endless days and nights, waiting for supplies, waiting to die. And so many did, so many. Yeah, everyone thought the war would end after D-Day. Little did those poor bastards know what lay in store for them.

Bobby had camped in winter before, hunting and such. Remembered one time they went to bed in a dry field, woke up with a foot of snow on the roof of the tent. Lucky for them, it was a big old canvas cook tent that held the snow off pretty well. Not that this little nylon one wouldn't do the same. It would just slide off of it, that's all, that's the difference.

Once he got the camp set up, he opened up the old Coleman stove and got it going for some beans. Lot a people thought it was the right thing to do to put a can of beans right in the fire. Well, that probably worked fine for those old Texas rangers, but why the hell would you want to burn your hand off trying to get it out of the fire. No, not him. Roughing it was one thing. He'd done plenty of that in his life, what with Nam and all. He was as tough as any of them—just not as dumb. Or was he?

He tossed a few logs into the fire pit and gathered up an armful of sticks from around the wooded area. He threw a few handfuls of pine needles and pinecones on top. Tearing a few strips off the newspapers he had brought along, he lit them up. The fire caught, and a blaze followed just like he knew it would. Meanwhile, he got himself pretty organized and tore open the package of hotdogs, sticking a couple on one of those old-fashioned hotdog sticks with a two-pronged fork at the end. He leaned it against the rocks around the fire pit, making sure it wasn't too close to the flame. Blackened was one thing, charcoal another. He stretched open his lawn chair and settled in next to the fire with another cold beer and his bottle of Jack on the ground next to him.

When the beans bubbled, he opened the bag of hotdog buns and pulled two off the bunch. He spread them open and pulled the dogs off the stick with the open buns. Grabbing a paper plate, he took them, the bag of chips, and the pan of beans over by the fire. He loaded the hot spicy mustard on the dogs. Damn, no onions. Should have remembered the Goddamn relish, too. Oh well.

No ketchup though. He never had gotten next to that idea. Sandy, man, she loved ketchup on her hotdogs. Said her mother made them that way. It took her into her twenties before she could stand mustard. Bobby, he thought it was a crime to desecrate a good dog with ketchup. Ruined it, plain and simple. He shoveled in a few mouthfuls of beans and washed them down with beer.

The hotdogs disappeared in three bites, each followed by a few handfuls of chips. Bobby cracked another beer and finished the beans with a belch. He wiped his mouth on his sleeve and rubbed his hands on his jeans. The Jack Daniels beckoned, and he took a couple of pulls off the bottle, sighing deeply, enjoying the heat in his belly and the warmth from the fire, which had settled into a low flame.

He secured the food in the cab of his truck before taking one last look up into the night sky and crawling into his sleeping bag. It was a cold night. It took him a few minutes to warm up the bag and get some circulation into his feet. His mind ran through the events of the last few days for about the thousandth time while he awaited the welcome respite of sleep.

It wasn't until the next morning that he realized he'd forgotten to feed the Goddamn dogs! Well, they'd make it, they'd been eatin' on the bones of that fucking elk he shot all week, they'd figure something out. His dogs had learned to be mighty resourceful given his general lack of interest in them and their freedom to roam. There were lots of little critters out there that they could catch. Hell, he'd seen one of 'em pounce on a squirrel and snap its neck so fast it would make your head spin. They'd be fine, he thought, trying to put the extra worry out of his mind. Bobby slept pretty well that night considering he was lying on the thin foam, but worry and fear have a way of bringing on exhaustion.

Whup, whup, whup. That damn dream woke him up at dawn. He ached from head to toe and sat up stretching his lower back. Twisting from side to side to loosen his muscles and joints, he crawled out of the bag, found his boots and pulled them on before he crawled out of the tent into the chill morning air. Damn if it didn't smell good. Nothing like the smell of pine and the rich, musky smell of the dried leaves and autumn brush. He stood for a moment gulping deep breaths of the fresh mountain air and checking out his surroundings.

Then he got down to business and looked around his campsite for some kindling. He gathered a decent little pile that would get him through breakfast and the rest of the morning. He stacked the kindling in a little pyramid along with some dry grass and leaves. It caught flame quickly and before he could get the coffee pot ready, he loaded in his firewood and had a good little fire blazing in the pit.

He sat down in front of the fire. He had to admit, whoever invented the fold-up, nylon chairs with the place for your beer had to be a genius. Shivering as the warmth of the fire crept up his legs, he rubbed his hands together. He gradually relaxed. Just about the time his jeans were hot enough to burn his legs, the coffee boiled. Drinking it greedily, he relished the heat as it rolled down his throat into his belly.

At certain times of the day, he could pick up local channels on his transistor radio. He listened as he made breakfast but heard nothing about a missing person. He kept busy by gathering and chopping some additional firewood and straightening up the campsite. The first day, he took his bow and arrow and hiked down into a rocky area where he thought he might bag some sort of wildlife, a rabbit at least. He was awfully tempted to poach a deer, but a little worried about attracting attention or getting picked up by the cops. He found a spot where he had a superb view of the tall peaks, their summits suddenly dressed in snow. He nestled into a spot in the rocks where he could watch the area unobserved.

Before he knew it, a brown rabbit had ventured out into the open, its nose and whiskers twitching as it munched on tufts of the green grass that remained here and there. Bobby lifted his bow and straightened the arrow he had already nocked in place. He drew back and aimed. The arrow released with a twang and flew straight and true, catching the critter in the head.

The arrow pinned it to the ground, not that it was going anywhere, and Bobby clambered down the rocks to retrieve his prey. It was a little rabbit, but it had enough meat for dinner and Bobby loved rabbit stew. He removed the arrow and lifted the rabbit by the back feet, wrapping some twine around them to hang it up from a tree until it bled out. Meanwhile, he sat back down and cracked a beer he had stowed in his pack. It had gotten a little warm, but that never bothered Bobby. Oh sure, cold was better, but beer was beer.

As he walked back to camp, he pulled up a handful of wild onions he found growing in a dry, sunny spot or the shoulder of the mountain. The blossoms had faded and dried, but the onion still had some meat to it. It was strong and tasty and would add some flavor to his stew.

He skinned and cleaned the rabbit once he got back to camp and stuck it in a sealable plastic bag in the cooler until he could get the fire built up. He could have used the Coleman stove, but somehow, food cooked over an open fire always tasted better.

By the fourth day, he was getting antsy. He'd stayed up half the night before with the lights, trying to contact other life forms, but he only saw one bright light hovering at a distance. He couldn't get the damn thing to come any nearer, no matter what signals he sent.

Bobby packed and headed home. As he neared his gate, he spotted a Deputy Sheriff waiting for him. This was it. Time to face the music. He headed toward the deputy who had parked at his gate. He pulled up, opened his window and asked how he could help the deputy. They both entered the property through gate and headed toward the house. Bobby prayed he had not left any evidence. But as they pulled up and they both saw the dog with the severed arm, Bobby planted the kick to the deputy's groin and made it inside his house. The seige was on. The deputy.

,

,

,

,

,

,

,

,

,

,

,

UNDER SEIGE

D eputy Dinkle hobbled to his cruiser and raised the alarm over the radio. "10-67! I just found a dead body! The suspect is holed up!" he shouted into the radio. Then came the call. "APB! A 10-67 in Long Bow. A suspect is under siege in the area three miles south of Highway 285 on Eagle Valley Road." Jason Parks pulled out of the police garage at the Taj Mahal—the favorite but not the fondest nickname the residents of Jefferson County had dubbed the grand palace that housed all of Jeffco's support services. The courts were there, the assessor, the treasurer, and most important to Jason, the county jail sat across the street.

Jason heard the call and hit the gas, leaving black tire marks in his wake. He flashed momentarily on his date that night—that cute little Jody Vargas and her tight, round ass. Oh well, there'd be another day, another time. It could all just wait. He flipped on his lights and crossed Sixth Avenue doing 50, grateful the light stayed green. He took the entrance ramp to C-470, accelerating to 70mph and got in the left lane.

Jack Ruffien got the call near the end of his shift.

"Car 24, do you read?"

Possible 10-67. Dead body? The words that sent cops into overdrive. It blared over the radio and both Jason and Jack turned their patrol cars onto C-470, lights blazing, heading toward 285 at eighty miles per hour. They passed the Morrison exit in a minute and a half, blowing by Bandimere Speedway like a couple of their dragster drivers. The clock at the speedway said 3:18.

Jack raced up Highway 285, his adrenalin rushing wildly. "Yep, complete boredom punctuated with moments of sheer terror—what a thrill." He dialed his cell and then thought better—why worry Joleen, he thought, breaking the connection. Passing the exit to The Fort Restaurant, he barely gave it a look. Some years ago, he and others escorted the Presidential motorcade, guiding President Clinton and the leaders of the G8 Summit to the uniquely old west restaurant. In fact, the chairs the heads of state used that night now bore engraved brass plaques on the back of each with the name of the leader who sat there.

Jack had only been there twice himself, but it was definitely top drawer. Joleen arranged their 25th anniversary party there and, despite the cost, it had been great. Rocky Mountain oysters, rattlesnake hors d'oeuvres, elk and venison, quail and duck, all great game dishes superbly prepared. The owner was well known for donning a coonskin cap and knocking the cork out of a champagne bottle with a tomahawk. Quite a place. They designed it like an old fort, a fifteen-foot stucco wall wrapped itself around the place. Within those walls, a teepee stood tall, and, at one time, a bear sat in a large cage greeting the guests. (The PETA folks of the 1980s took care of that deal, though. The bear had been moved to a better lifestyle.) Now a small trinket and local jewelry and artisan shop commanded a pretty price instead.

Jack caught up with Jason as they headed deeper into Turkey Creek Canyon, his squad car moving at 80mph, blowing past the cars and trucks that pulled over once they spotted his flashing lights. This was a part of the job

Jack loved. A mission—some place to go, a big case, a bust, a takedown! Instead of the same old stuff, a traffic ticket, a neighborhood dispute. He pressed his foot down harder on the accelerator and blew by all those happy commuters. Sometimes he wanted to wave as he passed. But this type of call was troubling, the worst—possible dead body.

They flew through Turkey Creek Canyon in minutes and passed the Tiny Town exit, heading onto the flat of the highway. The Homestead Meadow went by in a blur, and they saw Pokey's in their rear-view mirror. Normally, it would be a place to stop for coffee and burritos at dinnertime, but today it was merely a landmark. They dropped down into Aspen Park and saw the famous Coney Island Hot Dog stand with a parking lot full of cars. It was one of the few unique landmarks, and it had been there forever, though rumor had it a bank would soon take its place.

It was a stucco building in the shape of a hot dog topped with mustard and relish. A couple of years ago, one end of the wiener had fallen off, but they had quickly repaired. It was known for the best, greasiest burgers in Jefferson County and foot-long hotdogs with as many chopped onions as a fellow could stand. And onion rings to die for, well, maybe not. Jack heard they listed it for sale for a million bucks! Hard to believe, since it could hold about six people in line at the counter and sported two picnic tables on a small deck outside.

They blazed through Conifer Junction and were nearing their turnoff where three cars had lined up in the turn lane. Jason wheeled around them, sliding in the pea gravel that covered all mountain roads from mitigation on past snowy days. Jack stayed close behind, barely missing a head on with a truck coming the other way. Goddamnit—didn't people see the lights! That's the bad thing—people oblivious to their surroundings, radio blaring, never looking in their rearview mirrors, out there in la-la land somewhere. They both knew the road. They'd patrolled it many times, though rarely for any kind of violent incident back that way.

The first patrol cars were already at Bobby's gate, which was secured with a thick chain and padlock. Jack's car made the turn onto the road and slid to a stop just inches short of the other patrol cars, throwing dust and rocks at Jason, who now followed close behind. Jack zigzagged to avoid the thick cloud and kept up his speed on pure faith. White fences and barbed wire flew by in his periphery. He felt like he was racing at Talledega, getting it on.

The lead officer stood popping the chain with a bolt cutter. He pulled the gates wide apart and yelled, "Go, just go. I'm right behind you."

Jack saluted and sped through the gate, leaving Jason eating dust. Jason liked dust. The four cars roared down the road, occasionally hitting bumps that left daylight between their tires and the road. They hit the curve at thirty, sliding sideways together, almost blowing over the ridge on the left, but pulling it out at the last second. Another law enforcement benefit—driver training. Jack pulled up and Jason parked next to him, gazing at the wagon wheels silhouetted against the setting sun.

They could see a lone Sheriff's patrol car parked at the side of the house. Jason got out of his vehicle and approached Jack's driver's door.

"Shit, what do you think, man? Is this another Ruby Ridge or what?"

"God, I hope not. Here comes a deputy. It's Dilbert, I think. Why's he walking like that? Dilbert!" he whispered sharply. Dilbert lurched toward their cars, one hand clutched around his balls.

"Motherfucker kicked me in the balls. Shit, guys, there's a bloody arm laying back there in the grass. This guy's some kind of freak!" Jason stopped and held his scrotum lovingly.

"He alone?"

"Yep."

"Okay, Jason, let's move in. Get your shit."

Jack and Jason struggled into flak jackets and clipped tear gas canisters onto their belts. Jack pulled the shotgun out of its position and cocked it. Jason secured his Kevlar vest and grabbed his automatic rifle, patting his revolver and stuffing his pockets with ammo clips. Ought to be enough, he thought. They moved their cars into defensive positions and got back out. Jason glanced over his shoulder and saw Jack motion silently, "This way." They crouched behind one of the cars and watched. In a moment, three more squad cars arrived and before long, an NBC satellite truck pulled in.

LOCKED AND LOADED

O nce Bobby incapacitated the deputy, he got inside the house and set the alarm system, hurried to his bedroom and pulled back the rug that covered his gun safe. Lifting the hatch, he yanked the heavy bags filled with guns and ammo out onto the bedroom floor. He started loading his weapons, beginning with the banana clips for the AK's and H&Ks and grabbed some extra clips, too.

He strapped on his body armor and slipped his shoulder holster on with the 9mm and stuffed some full clips into his pockets. He glanced out the window again and spotted the cop on the radio, hunkered low. Placing the weapons at strategic locations, he carried several up the stairs where he positioned himself in the upstairs bedroom with a bottle of Jack and a half-smoked reefer and waited.

His body shook like crazy, and he took a couple of pulls off the bottle to calm his nerves. The dogs kept barking, and he leaned close to the wall and peeked between the shades in time to see the first of the Deputy's back-up gang arriving. Despite the seriousness of his situation, Bobby couldn't help but chuckle when Deputy Dinkel hobbled over to them. After jawing for a minute or two, they all loaded up and crouched behind the squad car. Soon, three more vehicles pulled in and a whole shitload of cops in SWAT gear tumbled out.

They all gathered behind one of the cars and seemed to be making a plan. Bobby watched them as the split up and surrounded the house, creeping low and darting from one strategic spot to the next.

Suddenly, a plain-clothes cop in a shirt and tie pulled a megaphone from the trunk of his car. He leaned toward Deputy Dinkle who whispered something and then called out, "Robert, this is Detective McDonald. We don't want any trouble. Come on out now, and nobody will get hurt."

The sound echoed through the silent twilight. The silence broke again as Bobby fired a round through the little side window and the glass shattered, sending those boys diving for their cars. He had enough ammo to hold off a small army and planned to do just that. Te deputies hunched down and started running toward the house, and he knew they were looking for a way in.

Jack signaled to Jason, and they plastered their bodies against the side of the house, .45s in hand. The shot had come from the upstairs window. If they could get around to an entrance, they might get inside. They moved slowly, unsure of the capabilities of their shooter.

Bobby watched the two deputies move in. He slipped down the stairs quietly, knowing he would hear the security alarm sound and see the flashing light indicating which door they had breached. He fingered the trigger of his rifle and turned off the safety. He was ready.

Detective McDonald picked up the radio, "McDonald."

"Suspect has a felony menacing conviction in 1992, spent 2 tours in Nam as a Marine."

Shit. This was gonna be harder than he hoped. He picked up the megaphone again. "Robert, let's end this now. You still have a chance. Put your weapon down and come out."

Bobby chuckled grimly. Yeah, right, that's just what I'm gonna do. He held his AK-47 with a full clip and stood by the security system monitor to see where they were coming in. He slipped over and turned the television on without the volume.

GAWKERS AND GUNS

John arrived at the gate just as three news trucks pulled in and CNN and Fox were right behind him. He'd seen the patrol cars fly past on the highway as he drove home, but never dreamed Bobby's place was their destination. The whup whup whup of a news helicopter circling overhead left a dull continuous thrum echoing in his ears. He had heard the news coverage on the radio and a deputy stopped him as he tried to drive through the gate.

The news channels broadcast the event live nationwide and on all the locals stations, reminiscent of all those crazy crimes scenes like the O. J. slow speed chase or the bank robbers in LA. That was the thing with 24-hour news, nothing went unnoticed, no crime scene was undocumented or unchronicled and the news networks rubbed their hands together with glee, rushing to get their people out there to report every movement, every word, every gunshot.

Now the reporters and cameramen lined up along the road between his house and Bobby's place, talking and filming continuously, while the producers scrambled for facts on the suspect and his background, his family, the property and any other good dirt or information that might propel the story forward.

A uniformed Sheriff's deputy held out his arm and said, "Sorry, no entry, this is an active crime scene."

"Well, I live back there."

"You related to Robert Truax?"

"Nope, he's my neighbor. I live down the hill past him."

"Do you know him?"

"Little bit, like neighbors do."

"Think you might help us calm him down and get him to surrender?"

"Whew. Not sure that I'd have much influence on him. I barely know him. Have you talked to his ex-wife?"

"We're contacting her now."

"Well, I'd say she's your best bet for influencing Bobby. He's a strong-headed guy, and he's not afraid of anything."

"Okay, will you stand by in case someone wants to talk to you?"

"Sure," John said, seeing as how he had little choice in the matter. The officer waved John through, and he headed down the road until all the people congregating in the road and the cars and vans and satellite trucks parked blocked him.. He pulled over and got out. He had a clear view of Bobby's house.

It was dusk now, and the house sat in total darkness, but the cops had set up spotlights shining on all sides hoping to illuminate the inside of the house and either intimidate or get a shot at Bobby. John heard a loud voice over a megaphone, and though he couldn't make out the words real well, he had a pretty good idea of what he was saying.

Cop Killers Don't Go Free

Ruffien and Parks were no dummies, and they could see the security wiring on the windows and knew he could track their entry through it, but they took a chance anyway and busted one window on the front porch with the butt of an assault rifle. Jason broke out the remaining shards of glass that rimmed the frame and put one booted foot through when Bobby got to the doorway facing the porch. Ruffien stood behind with his service revolver aimed through the window for cover.

Bobby stood in the shadows and saw the leg come through. He let the assault rifle hang at his side and pulled the .45 from his holster and took aim at the cop. Holding the gun with both hands, Bobby blew off the side of Jason's face in a fury that sent blood and bone and teeth spraying over Jack. Jason fell backward and Ruffien dropped to the ground for cover. Bobby backed up behind the wall, out of sight. He knew it was all over now. Cop killers don't go free.

That's when all hell broke loose. Bullets rained through the windows, but by now Bobby positioned himself near the massive fireplace and hunkered down low.

About this time, the SWAT team moved in close, and the news crews tried to do the same, but the cops kept them back with a crime scene tape along the road. That and standing there with their arms spread to ward them off, but those folks are persistent as hell and have right to be there. So, they were pretty well ensconced on the road.

Now you got to remember, sound travels through those canyons, and before long, neighbors were coming from every direction and gathering on the hillsides, clutching their jackets around them and holding their dogs and kids back, but they sure as hell wanted to see what was going to happen.

The police negotiator worked hard to reason with Bobby again over the megaphone, and John saw him using a cell phone, too. With the windows busted out, the shrill sound of Bobby's phone ringing echoed though the evening air, but he never answered to the guy on the megaphone or picked up the telephone, which just kept ringing. Could have been the cops or somebody he knew calling to talk him out of the mess. He just kept firing rounds each time they called to him. John got up as close as he could and saw a cop coming toward him to push him back.

"Hey, I'm a neighbor from just down the road. What's going on here?"

"We found body parts in the yard, and Truax is a suspect for the murder. Now he's holed up shooting cops left and right. Do you know his family?"

"I don't think he has much family and don't really know him that well myself." John was hoping not to have to compromise his relationship with Bobby, no matter what he had done. Might have been stupid, but he was brother of sorts, Vietnam and all.

THE SMELL OF CORDITE

B obby moved around the main floor and was running mostly on adrenalin by that time, darting around from place-to-place, firing when need be, taking swigs of whiskey in between, which made him even crazier. Whup, whup, whup.

As more cops arrived, they scrambled to put on their body armor and moved around behind their shields when ambulances started rolling down the road, sirens screaming and lights flashing and causing an even bigger ruckus. Folks in those parts had never seen anything like it, and the crowd kept growing.

News people and cameramen were running all over the place looking for interviews and photos.

Four SWAT team guys crawled through the tall grass on their bellies, moving toward the side door. They rose to crouched positions on either side of the door. They didn't know Bobby could see them from the window, and he took aim with his pistol. He blasted two of them, who fell into the stack of dog food bowls and trash stacked alongside. Dog food flew in every direction and garbage blew out of a big black trash bag. Cans and beer bottles and discarded food stuff flew in every direction, littering the grass.

One SWAT guy lay writhing in the mess, bleeding profusely from the shoulder where white bone protruded from the dark, red, shattered flesh. The sharp stench of spoiled milk filled the air. They heard the moaning and screams of the injured cop. "I'm hit, I'm hit," he screeched. The other cop lay dying with a hole in his neck that almost severed his head, which now lay at a strange angle to his body. His eyes glazed, and the first spurts of blood had slowed to a trickle as his heart slowed and stopped pumping. His left hand twitched, and he opened his eyes real wide, falling still.

John heard the shots but felt pretty sure Bobby had fired them since the others hadn't moved in. The megaphone blared again. They waited a bit, and then a captain gave a sudden hand signal and fire rained upon Bobby's house. The smell of cordite hung heavy in the chilly air. A few more cops moved in close, and Bobby fired as they moved.

To the Rescue

To the Rescue

S andy sat on her sofa, mopping her face with a tissue
as she, Liz and the officer watched the coverage. He
pushed the off button on his cell phone and said, "They
think it might help. What do you say?"

"Okay, I can't stand to see more people die. I'll do
whatever I can. Liz may be able to help, too. Let's go."
She grabbed her jacket and purse and together they went
out to the patrol car. She rode in the passenger side.

"It's so sad. I love Bobby, but so much stuff happened
to him that changed him until he's no longer the man I
knew and married. He's so angry and bitter, especially
since little Bobby died. That did it for me. I couldn't bear
it any longer. I guess he couldn't either."

"Have you talked to him much recently?" Liz asked.

"Yes, we've been trying to get back together. That's why
I think I might calm him down—and why I'm so shocked."

Just then, her cell phone rang. "Hello? Oh, hi Tim. God,
do you believe this? Yeah, I'm on my way there now.
They want me to try to talk him out of this mess. I'm not
sure, you know Bobby. Very little alters his state of mind,
don't know that I can. Okay, well, I'll see you there. Is
everything okay with you? 'Kay, bye."

She glanced at the officer and said, "Old friend of Bobby's. He's up there now, but the cops won't let him near. He's probably as good a bet as any for getting to Bobby. They should let him talk to him."

The cop picked up his radio and relayed the message.

REALITY BITES

C arolyn Wafer sat on the couch biting her nails and wiping the tears that ran in rivulets down her swollen cheeks. It seemed obvious Tom was dead, though no one confirmed it. It had to be him—a revenue officer? No doubt. Of course, she prayed and hoped it was all a big mistake, but in her heart, she knew the truth. Her parents had called earlier and were on their way over. She sat in the dark room illuminated only by the flickering light of the television screen where the reporter's voice droned on and on, repeating the same information over and over and over. God, she wanted to scream. She pressed her hand to her abdomen and more tears streamed down her face.

Last Ditch Effort

John stood watching the melee and turned to see Bobby's friend Tim approaching on foot on the road behind him. He raised a hand and nodded as he walked up.

"Hey, Tim, how'd you get in?"

"Crawled over the fence up above." I nodded. "Fuckin' Bobby, man, what's he doing? They're gonna kill him." John nodded grimly.

"Think he killed that dude?"

John shrugged. "Hard to say. He sure has the firepower. I guess they're saying it was a revenue agent—IRS. I know he hated those guys with a passion. No telling what could have happened." Tim shoved his hands in his jean pockets and nodded sagely. He, of all people, knew Bobby's attitude about most things.

"Sounds like they're bringing Sandy up in a patrol car."

"You're kidding. For what? To talk him down? Think it'll work?"

"Might. He still loves her. God only knows."

Then a car began crawling toward them from the direction of the gate, and they could see by the bubble gum lights on top. It was a squad car. As it approached, they could make out the image of a somber-faced woman with blonde hair in the passenger seat and another woman in the rear.

Tim waved. "It's her and Liz! Shit, I hope this doesn't get too nasty—like it ain't already."

Down below, they could see the cops were getting the tear gas canisters ready, donning their gas masks and all. But they both knew Bobby was well-equipped and would have his own gasmask on in a matter of seconds. They saw them raise the first canister to pitch through the front window when a loud megaphone blared. "Hold up." They lowered the canisters and turned as Sandy, Liz, and cop turned down the drive toward the house.

A murmur ran through the crowd. "It's his ex-wife. It's Sandy."

The car rolled to a stop about fifty feet away from the building, and Sandy emerged. She wore slacks and a white blouse with a plaid jacket. There was a sadness to her eyes and a weariness to her demeanor. The officer led her toward the negotiator with the megaphone.

Sandy Speaks

B obby saw the headlights flash across his walls and peeked through the corner of a window. Shit. It's Sandy. Now what the fuck did they bring her up here for? Goddamnit! Moving away, he slumped against the rock wall of the fireplace. He knew he had some time as they set her up with the phone calls and megaphone, Reloading his .45, he checked his clips for the assault rifle. He crawled to the coffee table where he had a half a reefer and lit it, sucking hard. Instant relief washed over him, and he took a couple more hits before he laid it in the ashtray, watching the flame die as the smoke curled up and disappeared.

After another swig from the bottle of Jack, he crawled to the kitchen and pulled the plug on the refrigerator so the light wouldn't show when he opened it to grab a beer. He popped the can and poured the cold liquid down his throat, sighing as he lowered it. After two more long swigs, he cast the empty aside as he crawled back into position with his AK across his lap and his rifle at his side. The television coverage showed Sandy and the negotiator in heavy conversation.

An ambulance was putting the finishing touches on one of the dead deputies and rolling his body bag into the back of the vehicle for transport to the morgue. A reporter stood blabbing endlessly outside his house live on camera with the spotlighted house in the background. He shook his head in wonder. How the hell did I get into this fix, anyway? Goddamn IRS! The past week seemed like a year ago now, and the burial of the revenue agent was a mere blur. Bobby took another swig off the bottle. The steady din grew louder outside, rattling his brain. Whup whup whup.

"Bobby, this is Detective McDonald. We have Sandy out here. She has something to say to you."

Bobby fired a round through the ceiling in response.

"Bobby." It was Sandy. Shit. The last thing he wanted was her involvement in this. She'd been through enough already. He felt like he ruined her life. "Bobby, it's me, Sandy. Don't do this, come out now. Don't hurt anyone else. End it here, please, please for me, do it, do it for us. It can't end this way, just come out now. I love you!"

He fired another round through the ceiling and saw Sandy hand the megaphone back to McDonald on the tube.

"Bobby, this is McDonald again. I'm coming in, don't shoot." Ha! That's a good one, he thought. He positioned himself in the shadows of the room in sight of the side door and waited, rifle aimed. Then a shadow emerged. Bobby fired through the window, sending shattered glass flying through the night. The Detective ducked and ran.

Did they take him for a fool? Did they think he was stupid? They'd find a way to shoot him dead the minute he showed his face and call it defensive action. He took another swig. His vision blurred and ears rang loudly in cacophony of racket. Can't go out there, can't do it, don't wanna do it, a voice screamed in his ears.

Suddenly he saw rushing shadows around the windows and lifted the assault rifle to his side and fired at 70 rounds per second sending a spray of bullets across his west wall. Jack Ruffien took a round in the thigh. His leg collapsed within his pants leg and blood ran into his socks. He fell, screaming in pain and held the stump of his leg moaning and grimacing.

Two deputies rushed in and dragged him out to the road where two paramedics cut away his pants and staunched the massive bleeding with a tourniquet and placed his severed leg in a bag with ice and then into a cooler. They strapped Jack down and hooked up IVs all at once. They rolled him onto a board and transferred him to the gurney which they loaded into the ambulance standing by. A thick, red puddle of blood soaked into the dirt of the road and turned it a muddy black. The ambulance flicked on its lights and sirens and headed out, moving at a pretty good speed, considering it was a dirt road and all.

All watched as the reporters scrambled to get good footage and poked their microphones into the faces of the bystanders looking to get the scoop on Bobby. Tim and John just played dumb but could hear one woman behind them granting an interview.

"Yes, she said. "I knew him well." Tim and John both whipped their heads around to see whose voice it was. If it all weren't so awful, they would have laughed. She looked about seventy with blue hair and red lipstick bleeding into the wrinkles around her mouth. Her dentures clacked together as she spoke.

"He was a very strange and violent man. We heard gunshots coming from his place all the time. One time I saw him at the mailboxes, and he growled at me like an animal. He killed his own son, you know."

Tim looked at John and rolled his eyes, but somehow they could both picture Bobby growling at her just to freak her out. She was probably staring at him. Tim spoke softly to John. "We knew a guy once in high school named Jerry. He was huge guy with a wild brown afro. His eyes rolled around in his head, and he drew all sorts of stares, but few dared comment. One night we all went into McDonald's and the usual stares ensued. Jerry hunched his shoulders, leered at the crowd and stuffed an entire hamburger into his mouth with a vicious growl. It was hilarious, but it scared the shit out of everyone there."

They both laughed but knew there was nothing funny happening.

COLLAPSE

C arolyn Wafer's mother sat next to her on the sofa cuddled up with her arm around her daughter, hugging her to her chest like a child. Carolyn's tears had dried up, and she sat staring numbly at the scene unfolding on the television screen. The ambulance was pulling out, driving through an unimaginable throng of curious gawkers that had gathered along the road. It must be pretty cold up there, she thought. People were hugging sweaters around their bodies and zipping up their jackets. Funny, it was still hot in Denver, but the 3300 extra feet of elevation turned even warm summer nights cool once the sun went down. The non-stop chatter of the reporters drove her crazy. She stood up, stumbled into the bathroom, vomited, and collapsed on tile floor.

FLIGHT FOR LIFE

J oleen Ruffien was dialing Jack's cell phone when she
saw the ambulance pull up near a cop who was being
dragged down the road by two others. Oh, God! It's Jack,
her mind screamed. She stood close to the television,
staring at the scene, and swallowed hard to hold back
the tears and the fear. *Please God, don't let him die*,
she pleaded. She grabbed her portable phone and dialed
dispatch.

"Dunlap here."

"Bob, it's Joleen Ruffien. I think Jack's been hit up at
that nightmare in Long Bow. Where will they take him? I
have to get there."

"Oh, Jesus, Joleen. Hold on, let me see if I can find
out." He put her on hold. Joleen couldn't take her eyes off
the television screen, but her mind ran wild. He couldn't
die. Not now, not when they were so close to retirement,
when she could finally have him to herself without the
daily fear of what might happen to him.

"Joleen, looks like they're going to Swedish by Flight
for Life. He's okay—it's his leg. He should be there in
about twenty minutes.

"Thank God," she sputtered. Grabbing her coat and purse, she ran out the front door and jumped in her car. The kids! She speed-dialed Tommy.

"'Lo."

"Tommy, it's Mom. Have you been watching the television?"

"Yeah, Dad's not there, is he?"

"He's been shot. He's on his way to Swedish on Flight for Life. I'm going there now. Call Ricky and come down at once. I don't know how bad it is. They said it's his leg. I'll call you when I get there. See you in a little while."

"Okay, Mom, we'll be right there. Don't worry, he'll be okay," he said encouragingly, but his heart was racing.

Joleen clicked the off button and backed out of her driveway, flipping on her headlights. She blew through the stop sign at her corner and got on the main road. She thought she should be there by the time they arrived with Jack.

As she pulled into the parking lot near the emergency room of Swedish Hospital, she heard the whup whup whup of the helicopter blades *Thank God*. They'd gotten there pretty quick. She parked and ran across the parking lot, her heart pounding in her ears. . Thank God. They'd gotten there pretty quick. She parked and ran across the parking lot, her heart pounding in her ears.

"Mom!" She turned and saw Tommy running toward her. "I think they just landed on the roof!"

She reached for his arm as he approached. "I know. I heard them. God, I hope he's okay." She broke down, and a sob erupted from her throat.

"Mom, take it easy. It's gonna be okay. You know Dad, he's a fighter. We have to stay calm for his sake. We may see him in a few minutes." He hugged her around her shaking shoulders.

They entered the brightly lit lobby of the emergency room and approached the desk. The girl looked up and smiled. They told her who they were and why they were there. She made a quick phone call and said he was on his way down to emergency. Pointing to a row of chairs, she said, "Have a seat, I'll call you when they bring him in."

Just then, Joleen looked down the hallway to her left and saw two cops and four attendants rushing a gurney down the corridor. The sheets covering the patient were soaked in blood.

"Oh my God, Tommy, look!" They stood up and started down the hall.

"Mom, Tommy!" They turned and saw Ricky running toward them. "What happened? Where is he? Is he okay?"

"Come on. I think he's down here," Tommy said, moving quickly. They caught up with the gurney just in time to see Jack's gray lifeless face disappear behind a set of swinging doors that said, "No admittance."

"Joleen?" She turned and saw one of the uniformed officers hurrying toward her.

"Oh, Dave, I'm so glad you're here. How is he? What happened?"

Dave told her what he knew, omitting the fact that Jack had lost a lot of blood, and they weren't sure they could stabilize him. Neither did he tell her Jack's leg was in a cooler.

"I think he'll be okay, Joleen. This is a great trauma center. The best. They'll do everything possible."

They went back to the emergency waiting area. Dave brought Joleen a cup of coffee, and they all sat together, waiting with dread at what might come.

Alien Rescue

B obby saw the flashing blue and red lights and knew they were hauling somebody out. Four down, fifty to go. He'd go out in a blaze of glory, but he wouldn't go to jail. Running on adrenalin now and booze, he knew something was brewing out there. He watched the coverage and saw the SWAT team putting on gas masks. He grabbed his own and pulled it down over his head.

Tim and John watched from the road as the cops donned their gas masks again. Two of them grabbed tear gas canisters, lobbing one into the downstairs, the other through an upstairs window. They all stood alert and waited. Nothing.

"Fuckin' Bobby, man. He's got them pretty confused," Tim said with a sardonic laugh. "They're gonna have to take him out feet first, but he could hold them off for a good long time with that arsenal."

John nodded and winced as they heard the glass shatter. All at once, the cops raised their weapons in unison, aiming at both doors, but Bobby didn't come out, which really threw them all for a loop. The tear gas started seeping back out through the broken windows, and those outside without masks began coughing and covering their mouths and noses. Then they started running, choking and puking as they went.

Those that remained reshuffled themselves like a deck of cards and took cover behind vehicles and up against the house, considering their options. It was obvious Bobby wasn't coming out of his own accord. Then they saw Sandy get the megaphone again.

"Bobby, don't do this. Come out now, there's still time. You don't have to die. Come out now." She handed off the megaphone with sad resignation. She knew him too well to think he would come out, so she climbed into the cruiser that had delivered her to the scene.

By this time, Bobby was about half crazy, between the noise, the booze, the pot, the adrenalin and the bizarre circumstances in which he found himself. His mind whirled and swirled and took him back to Vietnam when he found himself in a similar fix on more than one occasion. Those times when all hope seemed lost, death was imminent, and he felt doomed. Then, just when enemy forces had him cornered with no way out, he would hear the roar of the bombers arriving to strafe the Gooks and allow him an escape route. Or a Huey would move in and pluck him from the jungle below, saving his ass once again. Whup, whup, whup. But that was all back then and not too likely to happen now. There was just no time left, *no time left for you. On my way to better things, I'll find myself some wings. . . .*

He lifted his gas mask long enough to finish off the Jack and lay back against the rock wall of the fireplace to wait, to wait for something more to happen.

The cops moved again and took up new positions. Just about the time it looked like they were fixing to send a couple of SWAT team guys through the windows, come hell or high water. Then they saw the lights. Of course, Bobby had been keeping an eye out himself, but he had the gas mask on and wasn't thinking too clearly, anyway. Whup, whup, whup. He was still trying to get an edge on the cops, and with all the noise and confusion outside, he couldn't hear much. But he did see the lights and watched them as they grew closer and brighter, and he could see the wind created by the craft hovering above. The dogs were out there shivering and quaking like always when the lights came, and Bobby knew this was his moment. They had come for him.

BAD NEWS

J oleen and the boys sat silently in the reception area of the emergency room, leafing through magazines and looking up each time the double doors swung open. Suddenly, a doctor in blue scrubs emerged and approached them. They all stood. "Are you the Ruffien family?" he asked.

"Yes, I'm Jack's wife, Joleen, and these are our sons, Tommy and Ricky." Handshakes all around.

"How is he, doctor?"

"Well, he's gonna be okay, but we cannot save his leg. The bullet entered mid-shin and shattered both bones. The damage to the tissue is too great and there's no way to reconnect the nerves or reconstruct the bone. I'm very sorry. "

They stood in stunned silence, and then Joleen emitted a deep sob. "No, no, no. Not his leg. Not his leg! God, no, no, no." She pressed her hands to her face and bawled, her shoulders shaking with each sob. Tommy's eyes filled with tears, which he brushed away as he put a consoling arm around her mother's heaving shoulders.

"Mom, Mom, it'll be okay. Dad's a fighter, he'll get a prosthesis, he'll be fine. They have amazing things now. Don't cry, Mom, please."

Ricky stood helpless, fighting back his own tears as the doctor said, "We're moving him to intensive care until we can get him stabilized."

"When can we see him?"

"He's in recovery right now. He'll be in his room in about an hour."

As they sat waiting, an ambulance pulled into the emergency entrance carrying a grief-stricken, dehydrated Carolyn Wafer. Her parents followed behind. She had an IV and an oxygen mask.

"Has she been eating?" the paramedics asked her parents when they arrived at her home.

"I don't think so. We believe her husband may be the revenue agent killed by that maniac in Long Bow. She's been distraught all week. Will she be okay?"

"Yes, we just need to get some fluids in her and get her strength back."

"She's pregnant. Will the baby be okay?"

"Most likely, but time will tell. Right now, she needs rest and nourishment."

Her parents nodded and took a seat near the Ruffien family to wait, not realizing they had both lost someone in the siege.

Seth Jacobson's next of kin, already notified of his death, were on their way to the morgue to identify his body.

Whup, Whup, Whup

Bobby crawled to the window and pressed his hands over his ears to stop the incessant whup, whup, whup. He was so drunk and high and on a mega adrenaline rush that he could not shut out the noise. He could see the craft hovering above, drawing nearer. The same lights he'd seen so many times were shining down upon the chaos outside. He went to the back door and followed the lights, and the craft hovered lower and lower, and Bobby knew they had finally come for him—just in time!

The door flew open, and Bobby ran out of the house as the ladder emerged, and he ran for it, arms spread wide, looking upward in search of a long, white face with big black eyes, the eyes of friendly aliens. He had almost reached the ladder when he realized it wasn't a UFO, and the cop in the helicopter above him took aim and put a bullet right between his eyes.

Bobby stood stock still for a moment and then staggered backward, falling to the ground with his arms and legs splayed. The impact blew the back of his skull off, which landed five feet away. Blood, bone, and gray matter spattered all over the grass behind him. He was dead before he hit the ground.

The crowd let out a collective gasp and the hoard of law enforcement officers raised their weapons and took aim. The negotiator held up his hand to hold their fire. Tim shrieked, "No, Bobby!" They heard the shot and saw Bobby stagger and flop to the ground. Sandy buried her tear-streaked face in her hands.

"Goddamnit, what the fuck? I can't believe it. Fuckin' cops, man," said Tim.

Well, the helicopter lifted off, and the dogs ran over and started licking Bobby's head, and the cops moved in and surrounded him. The press made a rush for the house, but the cops held the line. Television stations broke into scheduled programming to announce the siege had ended and the suspect was dead. Cable stations that had been following the events got their reporters on the air live.

"The siege that held law enforcement officers at bay for over four hours tonight has ended with the death of Robert Lee Truax, alleged murderer. The incident began when the Deputy found a body part earlier today after visiting the Truax home for routine questioning in the disappearance of Thomas Wafer, a resident of Lakewood Wafer was an IRS revenue agent employed by the Internal Revenue Service. Mr. Wafer was on a field visit to collect back taxes from Mr. Truax. The investigation will now continue into the whereabouts of Mr. Wafer, to whom it is believed the body part may have belonged. Here now is a statement from one of Mr. Truax's neighbors. Mr. Franklin, will you tell us what you know about Mr. Truax?"

An older guy in a plaid shirt and bad comb over stood in the bright lights with a toothpick in the corner of his mouth. "Well, I don't know that much, but I live up the hill over there, and I've seen him around a lot. He seemed somewhat strange to me. He wore that built up boot and all. I've heard a lot of gunshots from down there in the past, but I know nothing about this alleged murder they're talking about."

Tim and John inched farther down the road, trying to get in a little closer. Not sure why exactly, they both just had sort of a proprietary attitude. They were probably the only ones outside of Sandy who actually had spent time with Bobby and knew anything about him. Tim's cell phone rang.

"Yeah. Hey, yeah, I'm up here right now, saw the whole thing go down. He's dead, yeah. Blew the back of his head off. I know man, he was a unique individual. I'm gonna miss the dude. Yep, catch you later." He pushed the off button and looked at me. "That was Chuck. He and Nicky saw the whole thing on TV. Jesus, what a mess."

A few reporters moved down the road past the cops who held the rest of the crowd back. They were followed by cameramen who were itching to get a good shot of the body before it was hauled off to the morgue.

"I wonder how Sandy's doing?" John asked Tim. They heard later that she and Liz had sobbed when the bullet struck Bobby. She mourned while people all around the country cheered or cursed the police effort, depending on their point of view. But the loved ones of those involved in the siege heaved a huge sigh of relief as the debacle came to an abrupt end.

The cops left Bobby lying there in his own gore and entered his house. A few of the cops were working their way toward the house in a crouch, keeping their backs tight against it. They held their guns held out with both hands just like you see in the movies. They moved in and secured the house, cordoning it off with armed officers and yellow crime scene tape. Headlights flooded the windows until suddenly the interior lights came on.

About then, they saw headlights moving from the gate area and the Coroner's van passed by. Several people started sneaking around taking pictures and the coroner's people began to pick up the body parts and bullet casings and put them in brown paper evidence bags for later examination and identification.

Ever wonder about those brown paper bags we saw in the OJ fiasco? It seemed odd then, too. Isn't there a better way to preserve evidence than in a grocery sack? Maybe not, maybe plastic makes things spoil, go bad, rot, whatever, but it seems like banal methodology. Detectives walked around with brown paper bags collecting of evidence for later examinationget.

Plain clothes detectives had arrived quite a while before and took over, supervising the crime scene technicians who kept taking those brown paper bags out to the van. They likely tore that place apart before they were done and by first light when John left for work, most of the excitement was over.

Tim and John stayed until most of the crowd had dissipated after they realized they wouldn't get close enough to see the "good stuff." They saw Sandy roll past in the cop car on her way out. She and Liz both raised a slow hand in acknowledgment and shook their head side to side. Their faces were puffy, and their eyes were bloodshot.

Two more broken lives. It's sad when two people really love each other but just can't live together. Maybe if they'd stayed together Sandy would have been a stabilizing force in Bobby's life and none of this would have happened. Not to say it was her fault or anything like that, but it makes you wonder about the twists and turns of life and what effect they have on the end result.

John said goodnight to Tim and watched him walk out toward the gate. He got in his car and explained his way down the road to his house, showing his ID several times in order to justify his passage. He lay awake in bed that night thinking the whole thing over. He could just imagine Bobby inside that house. Funny, all that ammo and weaponry he had showed John that day actually did come in pretty handy for him. He never got to use the supplies he'd stored up, but that's neither here nor there. Seems like he knew he was going to need that stuff at one time or another. He was right.

The next day was Saturday, and everybody watched repeat coverage of the siege all day long on the tube. Found out that one cop had lost a leg from the knee down but would be okay. The rumors ran fast and furious as to the whereabouts of Tom Wafer. Later in the day, detectives revealed they had found the buried remains of Wafer's wallet and IDs along with the charred remnants of Bobby's bloody clothing. The clothing had been sent to some lab for DNA analysis to link it to Wafer.

Shovels and tools were collected as evidence and once daylight came, the ground around Bobby's house revealed dried blood and bits of human flesh. Things were looking pretty grim.

The detectives knocked at John's door early the next morning. The chain on the gate had been cut, and now it was open season. They asked everything they could think of to try to get information about where the body and the car might be stashed. John told 'em the truth.

"I don't have the faintest idea. I've been working a lot of overtime this week, got home and went to bed after a little tube time and a frozen dinner. Never heard or saw a thing. It's not like Bobby and I were best buddies or anything. I would have watched his dogs had he asked, but he wasn't that kind of guy."

A few days later, the arm was positively identified as Thomas Wafer's body part, and then the search expanded. Day and night helicopters flew over the property looking for a sign of freshly turned soil, a body or the little Escort. It wasn't until a week later that bloodhounds, following the scent from some of Wafer's clothes, led the authorities to the grave.

The dogs had done a thorough job of digging down, at least far enough to tear apart the black plastic and pull out his arm. The rest was up to the cops. They unearthed the black lump and got it to the morgue where Tom's mother and Carolyn went down to identify the body together. That's when Carolyn told her about the baby.

"If it's a boy, I'm going to name him Tom. If it's a girl, Thomasina. Oh, Betty, I don't know what we're going to do without him," Carolyn choked, trying to hold back the tears. Mrs. Wafer brushed the copper-colored hair from Carolyn's face and said, "We'll just take it day by day, Carolyn. That's all we can do."

Now they had the body, but the car remained elusive. There was a lot of territory to search, and those guys crawled all over that area for weeks. Finally a torrential downpour blanketed the entire front range. It rained for three days and nights and slowly the weight of the water began to pull the green tarp down the side of the Escort. The rocks rolled off and plummeted to the canyon below. The branches shifted leaving the windshield exposed to the sun's rays.

One day, a helicopter cruised slowly overhead when the co-pilot shouted, "There! I saw a flash of light! Circle back, and let's take another look. Sure enough, the Escort appeared, and they reported in. "I think we've got Wafer's Escort. It's sideways on a ridge up here above Truax's property. Gonna take some effort to get it out, but I'm pretty sure that's it."

Once they got in there on foot, they compared the VIN number and verified Wafer's ownership. John was sitting on his deck the day they hooked cables up to the car and lifted it out with a helicopter. They flew overhead and landed in Bobby's open field, lowering the car safely to the ground.

Of course, they found nothing to really tie it to Bobby except for fingerprints, but they already had all the evidence they needed. That pretty much wrapped up the whole ordeal, except for those whose loved ones were gone.

When it was all said and done there were five dead, including Bobby and the revenue agent. They had a big, televised funeral with uniformed police and state troopers marching in formation to honor the two state troopers and one deputy sheriff that lost their lives. A bagpiper played mournful tunes, and it ended with a twenty-one-gun salute.

Oh, it was all over the TV for days and covered from every conceivable angle right down to heavy psychoanalysis of Bobby and his motivation with some of those professional television shrinks who populate the tube nowadays during these kind of events. Even Geraldo Rivera got in on it and did an expose about the long-term damage of the Vietnam War on its Veterans. It was most likely just that Bobby simply was not about to be fucked with by anybody and was willing to stick to his guns, so to speak.

EPILOGUE

I t's John Tremont here. It's been three years now. The old place is still there, but you'd hardly recognize it. It sat empty for a long time. Tim called me after Bobby died and asked if I would help him and Nicki and Sandy clean the place out and get it ready to go on the market. So, I pitched in and, after a few weeks and two garage sales that attracted a lot of 'lookie lous,' we got rid of everything none of us wanted.

Sandy took his computer and sold most of the guns that Tim didn't want and the cops hadn't confiscated. I didn't take any, though they offered. Just didn't seem like a good thing to keep around. Not that I don't have a rifle and handgun for protection already, but it seemed like some kind of negative force to keep any of Bobby's arsenal. Sandy used what money remained, being the sole heir, to fix the place up enough to get it on the market.

The same gal that sold me my place showed up in her thousand dollars' worth of clothes and her Mercedes SUV to list the property. It took quite a while to sell, and a lot of folks just wanted to get a look inside the house of death, but the realtor was pretty good at screening them.

It seems nobody wanted to buy a place so tainted with blood and violence, but after enough time passed, some yuppies from California showed up and claimed they loved the privacy and isolation and saw so much potential. I met them at the gate to give them a key and make their acquaintance.

I have to admit, they got it at a bargain price, considering what homes in California go for, and they could put a lot of money into it. They gutted the place and changed the whole outside. They even have a lawn.

I think Sandy ended up with the dogs. I thought about taking them, but try as I might, I just couldn't get next to the idea. With the dogs gone, the only reminders are the occasional pieces of that crime scene tape I spot half buried or wrapped around the base of a tree.

I've done a lot of work on my own place, and now it's pretty darn tolerable. I installed a steel roof single-handedly using 4'x12⁄ sheets of steel roofing, which is a feat in itself on a pitched roof. The walls are finished in half logs, and it turned out pretty good. The old Westinghouse stove finally gave out, and I got a new refrigerator at the same time. Seemed like the right thing to do. Now, it's pretty presentable, and I've even brought a lady friend or two up for a visit.

I read recently that Carolyn Wafer remarried. Of course, it made the papers with a complete recap of the entire story. She married a doctor she met during the whole horrible event. I guess he looked in on her a lot, and then when she had the baby, he was the guy who helped her in delivery.

Jack Ruffien lived. Now he works with kids out at Craig Rehabilitation Center helping them learn to use a prosthesis. He even gets in a little golf. He retired on disability shortly after his recovery. I think he'd lost his edge. Can't blame him.

The shootout was all the folks in Long Bow could talk about for weeks, maybe even months, cause people just can't seem to get enough of that kind of stuff especially when it happens in their own back yard. It finally died down but even still, when the subject comes up, there's bound to be somebody who says, "That whole Bobby Truax thing? I'm so sick of hearing about that I could puke. But what do you think happened that day? That was so bizarre!"

I, myself, hardly hear a word about him anymore, but even to this day, sometimes late at night, I look up into the moonless sky, and think I see those bright lights, and I wonder if Bobby's up there somewhere looking down.

ABOUT THE AUTHOR

D enise Cassino has a BA in English from Northern Illinois University. She relocated to the Denver area after college and had a lifetime career in sales and marketing. Her first career was as a real estate broker in Denver, Colorado.

In 2009, Denise began a new career as an author, publisher, and book promoter. As a promoter, Denise has worked with more than 700 authors to successfully publish and launch their books to bestseller status on Amazon. She is also the owner of BestsellerServices.com, and DistinctiveYouMarketing.com. Denise lives in the mountains southwest of Denver with her husband and their four-legged friends. She has over 40 short stories and articles published in print and on the Internet, and this as her first novel.

Contact Denise at BestsellerServices.com
@denisecassino on Twitter
/DeniseCassino on Facebook
/DeniseCassino on Linkedi

.